HIDDEN SECRETS

HIDDEN SECRETS

J.S. Andersen

Idea Creations Press
www.ideacreationspress.com

Idea Creations Press
www.ideacreationspress.com

Copyright © J.S. Andersen, 2017.

This is a work of fiction. Any resemblance of characters to actual persons, living or dead, is purely coincidental.

ISBN-13: 9780997890426
ISBN-10: 0997890428

Printed in the U.S.A.

To countless friends, authors (you know who you are, Merri Halma, Lucinda Moebius. Not enough space to add them all), coaches (Leslie Silton), and editors who have helped me build my idea into a story. Of course, I can't forget my family and, most of all, my husband for putting up with my years of work and believing in me. And a big thanks to Dennis Young, my editor, who pushed me hard to finish this book.

Nampa is an actual city in Idaho, and the historical information is accurate, including the underground tunnels and the legacy of Bigfoot. The tunnels do not run miles out of town, but the stores the main characters go to existed, though today they have either closed or have been re-named.

The dirt pit existed until the late 1980s. When the irrigation ditch flooded into the pit, they filled it with dirt. There wasn't a tracker in the pit, but a car rolled down part of the side back in the 1970s.

Chapter 1

A few miles from Nampa, ID., Jim Forst woke as the Greyhound brakes squeaked, slowing down to take the freeway exit. A smell similar to burned peanut butter from the Sugar Factory raced up Jim's nose and triggered a gag. He looked at the white buildings covered with smog as the bus turned onto Northside Boulevard. Then, through open windows, a gust of wind brought the cherry on the top fragrance of heifers rolling in their manure.

Jim noticed a few new buildings combined with the familiar ones pass by as the bus slowed to a stop at its resting place on 12th Ave. In the fifteen years he was gone, the farm and potato town had grown little. He grabbed his duffel bag, nodded to the driver, and stepped into the passenger bay.

His old Ford truck's engine blew on his way up from Sierra Vista, Arizona. Bad luck followed Jim everywhere, and he hoped the family's hearse was drivable. He looked in Jenkins Antiques & Pawn Shop next door to the bus station to be safe. With good luck, he'd be able to pick up a used bicycle.

A pretty, red-headed woman carried out a bulky shabby chair and placed it beside the shop door as Jim approached. He studied her slim, shapely form as she went back inside.

He followed, hefting his duffle, heading for the door as she came back out holding a second chair of the same vintage. They collided.

"Sorry," she said, nearly dropping the chair on his foot.

"Let me." He set the chair on the sidewalk, smiled and held the door for her.

"How sweet," she said with the merest hint of a smile in her eyes. Jim followed her as she entered the store.

Wiping her hands on her jeans, she turned. "I'm Ruth." She held her right hand out.

He returned the offer. Ruth's slender hand was soft, and he felt the delicate bones through her skin. "I'm Jim." He wasn't worried about people recognizing him. Legally he was dead but it might have to get a fake I.D. before he came back. Heck, it was a last-minute trip with one change of clothes and no cheap cell phone. Jim thought the drug called Twist killed his brain cells for remembering things.

"Can I help you find anything?" she asked.

Jim scanned the room. "Got bikes?"

"Yes, but I don't have a big selection." She led Jim to the back of the store, where three bicycles rested on their kickstands.

He laughed and nodded at the first one. "I don't want a pink 10-speed and think the one with training wheels is small."

"The rusted one isn't too bad, eh?" Ruth gave him a playful smile and pointed to a faded blue bicycle with a few dark spots on the frame but otherwise appeared to be in good shape.

Jim noticed the flirt and felt her gaze as he squeezed the tires for air leaks. He relented and took a moment to consider what it would be like to squeeze Ruth and get into a cozy lip-lock with her. Nice.

He checked the price tag. Fifty dollars. "I'll take it." Jim took the handlebars and pulled the brake handles to test them. He didn't want to lock up in traffic and get killed for real. "Perfect."

Ruth rang up the sale at the register. "Are you new to Nampa?" and gave a hopeful smile. "I can offer a personal tour if you'd like."

"I'm here for a quick visit," he returned her playful smile.

She expressed a disappointed look. "A couple of days?"

"A few but busy."

Ruth smiled. "To be nice, I'll give you a break. With tax, it's fifty even."

"Thanks." Jim reached into his back pocket and took out two twenty-dollar bills and two fives. He knew one twenty was the real deal, the other a fake given to him by his handler.

Ruth lifted the bills one at a time toward the ceiling light. She squinted at the second bill and took her time examining it. She marked both using a felt-tip marker and put them in the cash drawer. The bill passed all of her inspections, like the one he used at the bus depot. His connection in the Cartel had perfected the skill of washing bills. Jim relaxed a bit.

"We set?"

Ruth nodded. "Yep. Enjoy your bike."

"I will," he gave her one of his better, engaging smiles. Jim adjusted the strap of the duffle bag on his shoulder, wrapped his hands around the grips, and pushed the bike out the door as Ruth followed, watching him pedal into the street.

When she entered back inside, Winnie, the store owner, came out of the office. "New man in town?"

"Oh, yeah."

"Noticed you had a pleasant chat with him. I didn't want to spoil it."

"I might have to track him down and give him a tour of our little burg." Ruth liked Jim's looks, wouldn't mind his brawny arms wrapped around her, and was positive his sea-blue eyes memorized her in return.

Both women smiled.

Chapter 2

The school bus honked. Melissa Mack, who everyone called Missy, flung a backpack over her shoulder, snatched two strawberry Pop-Tarts from the toaster, and ran out the front door. "Bye, Mom."

"Bye," Violet Mack, Missy's mom said.

The bus driver pushed the unoiled door open, a shrill shriek of metal on metal breaking the sound barrier. "You need to hurry faster, young lady."

Missy gave him a curt nod and headed down the aisle to her seat. "Dr. J is in a questionable mood today," she mumbled under her breath. She had given the bus driver the name Dr. Jekyll and Mr. Hyde two years ago, when she and her classmates started seventh grade, shortening it to Dr. J later.

"Back here." Maura waved her arms and gestured to the empty seat beside her.

The bus jerked as the driver shifted, causing Missy to lose her balance. Her hands landed onto a guy's chest she didn't recognize and pushed away before she face-planted onto his face. Missy made an apologetic expression at the red jam and crumbs smeared on his shirt.

"Sorry," she muttered and tried to wipe off the crumbs at the same time he brushed off what he could. Their hands touched.

"No prob," he grinned.

Missy drew her hands back and gave a remorseful smile in return.

Kaleb, who sat by the boy, saw the action and drew his mouth into its typical sardonic perverted look. "Nice way to start your morning, Miss Klutz. First the hurdles last month and now by your shoes."

She gave Kaleb a dirty look and wondered how his sister, Ally, could stand having him as a brother. Missy sat by Maura with the echo of Kaleb's smirks in her mind. Dr. J. permitted himself a snicker.

"Not a great way to meet the new guy," Maura uttered.

"New guy?"

"You'll find out soon." Maura scooted over on the bench, glancing up from her phone.

"Whatever." Missy wasn't in the mood to play a guessing game.

"Darn it," Maura scowled. "I've got duct tape on my butt. Stupid, lame seats." She lowered her head and continued to text. A few seconds later, she hit send. "One thing I've noticed throughout the school gymnastics team competitions is you didn't trip at all. We ended a month ago and you're tripping again. Why?"

Missy blocked out Maura's question about her tripping and looked at the surrounding seats. "Where's Ally? She gets on at your stop."

"She's PMing me back. Got into a tiff with her not-nice brother, Kaleb, and had trouble with her hair. She tried a new doo from a way-cool Pinterest blog and it went major wrong. She's not happy at all." Maura wrapped a length of her long, blonde hair around her fingers. "Her mom's dropping her off later."

Missy was glad she didn't have to worry about her hair. Brown shoulder-length hair wasn't a pain to style. Brush and let it hang loose or ponytail it. She dressed for comfort in jeans and a T-shirt, and she didn't know the meaning of make-up.

The bus came to another stop.

Julie huffed and flopped on the seat behind Missy. "Whew, just made it. I stayed up late riding my horse." She saw Missy crossing her legs, exposing her socks and grinned. "Stay up late too, I see."

Missy took a sniff at her armpits, knowing her clothes were clean. But not sleeping at night made her late with messy hair and bad breath.

Maura rummaged through her backpack. "Totally understand and love riding at night. My horse likes the dark and coolness." She got a ponytail holder from her backpack and handed it to Missy.

"Thanks." Missy pulled her hair back.

Julie pointed at Missy's feet. "Your socks don't match your shirt."

Julie was right. Missy always wore socks the same color as her shirts. "Brown's close to purple."

Maura looked over, "Why?"

"Why what?"

"Why'd you oversleep?"

Missy wasn't excited to tell her friends she had premonition dreams. They'd think I was a psycho lunatic. She simplified it. "Bad dreams."

"What?" Julie asked, leaning in closer.

Missy shrugged. She wasn't in the mood for everyone on the bus to know her business.

"What kind of dreams?"

Maura slapped Missy's arm, not giving her a chance to answer. "Now I remember,"

Missy jumped as a red mark in the shape of Maura's hand formed on her arm.

"Remember what?" Julie asked, looking past Missy at Maura with interest.

"Remember when I told you a new family moved into the neighborhood?"

"No." Missy was glad for the change of subject.

She pointed to the front of the bus. "See the boy sitting by Kaleb with pop-tart stains on his shirt?" Maura gave Missy a triumphant look. "His name is Brandon Miller. He's the one who moved into the house across the street from me."

Julie craned her neck to get a look-see as Missy shielded her eyes.

"Do you see him?"

"I see a dark-haired guy sitting there. So…" Julie pointed.

"Oh, man," Missy moaned. If I had my driver's license, I'd drive my motorcycle to school. I don't care if it's a dirt bike, I wouldn't have to deal with mental torture every day.

Maura fluttered her eyelids. "Wait until you see him up close. Brown eyes, cute face. AH." She licked her lips. "Check him out when we get off the bus." She paused. "And Brandon had a great welcome from Missy. She gave him a haunting thought every time he sees her in the neighborhood. Oh look, there goes the klutz." Maura laughed.

"How old is he?" Julie asked, knowing she needed to stay clear of the klutz subject.

"He's a sophomore." Maura smiled to herself. "A year older than us isn't bad at all, and I can tell he'll hang out with Kaleb. More pool time at Ally's house."

Julie shrugged. Missy knew Julie never hung out at Ally's house, and the pool time with the boys wouldn't change it.

Maura went on. "Speaking of pools, School's almost done and I hope Ally's parents open theirs early." She winked at Missy as she took strands of hair and wrapped them, again, around her fingers.

Missy could see it now: boy-watching. Ally would be much more interested in doing whatever her brother Kaleb did because it would be easier to follow Brandon around. Since Ally had a gigantic pool, most of the summer they'd be hanging around at her house. Maura and Ally were BFFs and expected Missy to tag along after them.

This was bad. Her social life was thin as it was. Missy's sole advantage was a small oval pool four feet deep and a trampoline. "But my pool will get deserted. It'll be sad and lonesome," she pouted.

Maura tucked the length of hair behind her ear. "Yep. But the prize, seeing Brandon in his trunks, will be worth it."

"Where is Ally?" Julie asked

"Having a bad hair day." She twirled her hair again. "Don't care."

True. With Maura, Missy never knew which way the wind blew. "You should stop twirling. One of these days, you're going to end up with a bald spot."

"Nah, I know when to quit."

We'll see. For a moment, Missy wished her a bald spot. A small one. She watched Maura look out the window, twirling. Missy didn't want to be like Maura, so she erased the thought.

The bus arrived at South Junior High. Dr. J. cranked open the door and maniac junior high juveniles piled out. Missy stood and yanked the notebook off the seat.

RRRRIIIIIPPPP.

Darn it. Duct tape from the seat found a new home and decorated her notebook. Nice.

Julie's eyes darted from the seat to the notebook, taking in the damage. "Not your day, is it?"

"Not even close," Missy grumbled and tore the sticky strip off her notebook. Half of the thin cardboard came with it. Nuts. She crumpled the tape into a ball and tossed it under the seat in front of her. "So, I'm a litterbug. Sue me."

Missy couldn't stop herself and glanced at Brandon and Kaleb as she walked by them. Bad choice. Brandon smiled. A smile added butterflies to Missy's stomach. Great, with her luck she'll trip again. She almost did and ran into Maura, who blocked the exit as she texted. "Move," Missy demanded.

Maura scowled. "Why don't you have a cell phone? Way uncool, you know."

She imagined Maura's thoughts. *Why are we friends? She's the weirdo of our group.'* And decided not to answer. Missy knew that if she did, Maura would give negative feedback. She wondered why she hung out with Maura and Ally. Being with Julie was fun, but the others came as a package deal.

Chapter 3

Jim biked south on 12th Avenue, turned right on 10th Street, and pedaled the last block to the front door of the funeral home. He dropped the heavy duffle onto the ground, sat back on the bike, and gazed at the old place. In the back of the lot and blocked off sight from the street was a single-wide trailer that had been his home from the time he was born through high school.

He remembered the day his grandparents told the family they planned to move to Arizona, where there was more business. They had a link for the Cartel across the Mexican border. The grandparents were in charge and his parents were the suppliers and deliverers.

Their cousin, Nate, would manage the Nampa funeral home as an in-between coffin hold- and delivery. Some people who died in Nampa wanted to be buried in a different state or vice versa when there was a real body delivery.

The good part of the plan was driving a hearse with a coffin full of drugs and not getting a suspicious look. His grandparents traveled to Mexico once a month to get cheap prescriptions and returned with uncut cocaine hidden in false compartments in their hearse. Once the drugs were in the States, they would ship them locked in caskets in the hearses to Nampa and other base funeral homes in the surrounding States. Border Patrol never searched his, and no self-respecting cop would lift the lid of a coffin and desecrate the body inside. Jim's mom told him at the start of the smuggling operation, the Cartel used to provide the bodies for his grandparents to transport in case the police became suspicious. Now they didn't even bother.

Several years ago, his grandparents and Nate created a new drug called Twist but didn't make it available until last year. They discovered if they blended a certain amount of Speed and Ecstasy, the user would feel good and not black out and forget. It was perfect to be on edge but still able to maneuver.

Rock's Edge, a gang in Caldwell, wanted in on the new drug distribution, with a fair share of the money. Nate said no, and all seemed fine. Two weeks ago, Jim's grandparents had come to Nampa to set Nate up with more supplies and the recipe to make Twist local; it turned out to be their last.

They had gone to make a delivery in the Caldwell area and never made it back. Rock's Edge had them cornered and shot. Apparently, the gang thought his grandparents and Nate had the car full of Twist. Wrong for both, and Rock's Edge went away empty-handed except for two pounds of Twist.

They shipped all three of the dead relatives back to Sierra Vista for a funeral. Jim wished his parents had come back to Nampa instead of him. It would be a lot easier for them. They were alive. For Jim, the place gave him nightmares. He hadn't heard if his parents or the Cartel made a threat or took care of the head of the group. Heck, Jim's parents didn't tell him anything of importance, only to do the dirty labor work.

With luck, maybe someone folded the recipe in the top drawer of the desk. If not, he'd get lost in a maze, trying to find it in a vacant field a few miles out of Nampa. His grandparents in the past buried coffins in the field, filled with equipment for processing the drugs, and who knew what else. Maybe the info would be in the shack by the field.

A school bus full of half-day kindergarten kids pulled up to the sidewalk and brought Jim back to reality. He watched the kids get off, laughing and talking. Jim wished his life was so simple. He rested his bike against the house and looked at the duffle bag. *When I leave this place, the bag better be stuffed with Twist and the recipe.*

With the heat, it was difficult to open the swollen door. But his metal shoulder was a handy tool to open anything. Jim didn't like the reminder of being rolled over by a tractor, tumbling down a steep hill. Soft dirt had saved his life, but not most of his arm. It limited his functions past normal usage, and he never felt pain because of the injured nerves.

He picked up the duffle and stepped into the foyer covered with plush green carpet that clashed with the pale

21

blue walls. A wanna-be artist painted four mournful doves on the wall in front of the couch, offering comfort to the bereaved. It looked too wishy-washy. His nose detected mold and dust, causing Jim to hate the place. Who'd want to spend time here, dead or alive?

His father's desk looked inviting, so he sat on the once-soft cushioned chair in front of it. On the left sat the same old phone, the answering machine beside it. Out of habit, Jim lifted the phone and heard the dial tone. It reminded him he needed to get a no-trace cell phone.

Jim put the receiver back in place and looked over the desk. Maybe they hid the recipe here. He fumbled through all the drawers. Loose papers, receipts, and empty Chicklet gum wrappers turned up. He swore at the desk: trash, useless trash.

He walked down the short hallway leading to a windowless garage and felt along the wall by the door frame for a light switch. The dark room brightened to a predawn haze as he flipped the lever. The dying fluorescent lights flickered in the ceiling.

A light-colored wooden coffin rested on the floor.

"Yahoo!" Jim smiled at no one. He unhooked the latches and opened the top half.

Nothing inside.

He opened the bottom part.

Still nothing.

He ran his hands over the black velvet fabric fitted to the inside.

Zilch.

At the upper end, in a corner, there was a little bulge in the pillow. He found a nail on the floor and used it to rip through the foam, looking for clues. It was empty. Jim loosened the material and gave a good yank. It came away from the glue. One more tugged and Jim tossed the fabric. His smile turned into a frown. A scrawny bag of drugs, not enough to get high, sat in the middle. He put it in his pocket and looked again.

Jim slammed the lids and bet his grandparents were laughing in their graves.

Checking all the shelves in the garage, he came across a large box. It sagged in on itself, sporting a torn flap. *Big enough to store something in.*

He lifted it off the shelf. It was heavy. With a couple of grunts, he carried it over and sat it on top of the casket. Inside, he saw an old cash register.

Yes. He straddled the casket and ripped the sides of the box open to get a better view of the machine. He tried the buttons, none of which worked, and ended up using the nail to pry in the register's drawer. He pictured money and more drugs in his hand, but when it opened, his reward was a dead spider.

Jim pushed the register on the floor along with the papers underneath it. He snatched the papers and thumbed through them one at a time. Trash mail. Old receipts. Sweat broke out on his brow.

Come on, come on, you old fart. Where did you put it?

He thought about throwing the pile of papers across the room or burn them. During one last look, he glimpsed blue pencil markings on the last crinkled sheet.

His heart pounded; he licked his lips. He yanked it out with excitement.

It was a map.

Chapter 4

Missy's teacher let them out ten minutes early from her second-period class. She stood by the wall beside the door for her third-period English class. Mrs. Buckner continued yapping to her captive audience. The bell rang and students filled the hall except Mrs. Buckner's. She sped up her words to get the last ones in before dismissing her class.

Missy shivered at a tingle on her neck. Ants? She reached under her collar to brush whatever it was away and felt fingertips. She turned and hissed, "Ally, quit it."

"Jeez, Miss, mellow." She stepped back. "You look a little lost."

"First, I overslept and had a spat with Mom. Next, Tommy spilled animal crackers on the bathroom floor and left behind some chewing gum, which I had the honor of adding to the bottom of my shoes. Then I mashed my Pop-Tarts as I got on the bus and ruined a notebook on duct tape. Enough for you?"

Ally shrugged, but Missy didn't blame her. Her list of complaints sounded pathetic.

The tardy bell rang and students flooded out of Mrs. Buckner's room. Missy and Alley waited for the doorway to clear before entering the classroom. They didn't want a head-on with another student.

"Good morning," Mrs. Buckner said as the students settled at their desks. "I know it has bored you going a week without homework, so today we're going to work on descriptive stories." She checked the clock before continuing to make sure all students were present.

"Open your English Books to page 98 and read through to page 101. Pick one topic for a descriptive story."

A small wave of groans rolled around the room.

Mrs. Buckner ignored the sound and proceeded to the whiteboard. "I want at least three pages and you can double-space." She wrote the page numbers on the board. "But I don't want large handwriting filling in the space. Example..." Her writing skills were sloppy.

"No copying. Use your own words." She took her seat. "Friday's the due date so work on it now. No excuses." She watched the students from her desk. "I want to see those hands moving, people." The teacher put on her glasses and took roll.

Ally leaned over. "Would a new hot guy in the neighborhood change your mood?"

"You mean Brandon?"

"News travels fast."

"Sure does. Julie and I got an earful from Maura on the bus. He sat up front so our view was the back of his head."

"When you see him, you'll know he's GQ all the way. Our whole family was over at their house visiting until late last night. Our dads are getting along like a house on fire."

"Brandon is friends with Kaleb?"

"He's been over there and they're hitting it off. So, yeah, I'll be seeing him a lot." Ally grinned and wiggled her eyebrows.

"Lucky you." Missy fluttered her eyelashes and puckered her lips.

"Quiet, girls," Mrs. Buckner ordered.

Ally and Missy straightened in their seats. Mrs. Buckner seemed mean and down-to-business, but she was a wonderful teacher. Plus, she said nothing about writing notes, so Missy passed one to Ally.

R u gonna chase after Brandon? He's gonna be at yr house a lot.

Missy dropped her pencil on the floor, picked it up and shoved the note under Ally's foot. Ally gave her a grin and retrieved the note.

"U-hmmm." Mrs. Buckner cleared her throat. "Melissa and Ally, you can stop the note-passing and do your assignment."

"Yes, Mrs. Buckner," they chimed together. It didn't stop their disobedience and Mrs. Buckner didn't care. Her expression was elsewhere reading a book.

Ally placed another note on Missy's desk. *Did you hear about Maura's past boyfriend, Vince? He got caught sniffing Twist in the boys' bathroom.*

Missy scribbled. *No flipping way. Bad stuff. It makes your brain go high speed.* And passed the note back.

Ally replied. *Ah yes, you know from experience.* She drew a face with a wink. Missy read the note and made a spacey face back. Mrs. Buckner glared at her again and the girls returned to their assignment.

Missy scanned over the pages of suggestions to base the description on. One was on flying. Her dad, Ray, had a plane and she had flown with him several times, but she didn't understand all the nit-picky stuff to describe.

Another topic frightened Missy of interpreting any dreams she had. Mrs. Buckner would think she was crazy if she wrote about a backhoe driving at night. The police and other authorities had looked into it, but they hadn't taken any action, yet.

Chapter 5

Jim hankered to go to the shack by the field but didn't feel like peddling the distance. Instead, he grabbed some junk food at a convenience store and lounged on the couch in the front office, staring at the map.

He got a pen from his duffle bag and marked the first place to dig for the coffins. Ten spots were spread around the field, and thankfully they weren't buried in the traditional six feet, but deep enough not to show by weather and natural changes.

Jim wished his cousin had left the hearse in driving condition. He remembered seeing a key in the desk drawn during his ransacking. He retrieved it, opened the back door in the garage, and froze. The trailer and the hearse were a sight to see. The trailer or what was left of it displayed Rock's Edge mark painted all over. They had hammered in most of the walls, shattered the windows, dented the doors, and broken the windows on the hearse.

Jim kicked a few more dents on the side to add detail. He couldn't think of another curse word bad enough to yell. He took the small bag of Twist out of his pocket and sniffed to take away his rage.

After a few minutes of looking inside the glove compartment, hidden pockets in the back, under the seats, and any place else he could think of, he went back into the funeral home empty-handed. No Twist.

I got to find where Gramps hid the Twist recipe, or I'll end up living with my parents for the rest of my life. A disaster. He couldn't leave Nampa empty-handed this time.

After a lousy night of sleeping on the couch, Jim was ready to trash the bike. No more carrying groceries on the handlebars. He peddled six miles to West Nampa, to a car lot. The place had seen better days, but at least it was still there and in business. Jim had noticed it as the Greyhound bus he rode on passed it the day he arrived.

The day was warm; the sun was bright. He felt a little sweaty as he kicked the stand down on his bike outside the small office. As Jim strolled around the lot checking out the cars, a husky man spotted him and headed over. The man stuck his hands in his pants' pockets, playing it cool. "Not too much of a selection, but they run." He stopped in front of Jim and held out his right hand. "I'm Dwight."

"I'm Matt. Looks don't matter as long as it runs."

"Any particular style?"

"Not picky."

"Over there." Dwight pointed to the far corner of the lot. "Tan, four-door Chevy Cavalier." They headed over to it. "They're built to last. A couple of small dings, but overall, it's decent." Jim knew Dwight couldn't overplay his hand.

Jim paced around the car.

"Door's unlocked."

He opened the door and slid into the driver's seat. He smelled a trace of stale cigarette smoke and opened the glove box. Empty. He got out and checked the tires for bulges.

"Want to see what's under the hood?" Dwight smiled.

"No surprises?"

"No." He reached into the car under the steering wheel and popped the handle to open the hood. "This is Idaho. People go deer hunting. I don't want to find myself slung over the hood of someone's pickup if I sold their kid a bad car."

"Keys?" With luck, there wouldn't be any. He wasn't in the mood to hot wire the car. He put his hands in his front pockets.

Dwight reached into his pocket, his hand coming out empty. "Be back in a sec." He jogged over to his office. On the way back, he slowed to a speed walk. New sweat stains showed up on his shirt underneath his suit jacket.

"Here you go. Want a test drive?"

"No." Jim held out his hands for the keys. He got in, cranked the motor, listened to the idle, revved the engine, and turned it off. It sounded smooth and he crossed his fingers there was no exhaust leak. Good enough. He got out and used the key for the trunk. Inside were a jack and a spare tire. Not bad.

"Price?"

"$500.00, if you got the cash," Dwight said.

Jim paused. He wanted to let Dwight think he had earned the sale. "Good 'nough." They went back to the office and Jim smiled his first smile.

"Hate these dang chairs." Dwight sat in a creaky swivel chair. He offered Jim a metal folding chair with no padding on the seat.

He knew the car lot didn't thrive and smelled it. Didn't matter to him. He needed a working car.

Dwight grabbed a pile of forms from a card table sitting at the side of the desk. "Need your driver's license." He looked Jim over. "Department of Motor Vehicles gives you a four-week grace period to register the vehicle."

He nodded. Being stopped for an expired temporary plate would put a spanner in his plans. "Fine."

If he hadn't found his items in a couple of days, he'd register the car. Jim thought maybe he could get a plate from Dwight. Do some bargaining because he felt a connection.

Sitting on the uncomfortable chair, Jim got his wallet and gave Dwight his license. *Here will be the test. I still don't have my fake I.D.* and counted out five-hundred-dollar bills. Dwight checked out Jim's license and made a photocopy of it as well as the five Benjamin's. "Gotta take a picture of the money since it's a cash sale." Jim's smile had been a brief one. He was back to business.

Dwight sighed and smiled nervously. "Never know if this copier is going to work." He opened it and took out the bills.

"Sign by the 'x's." Dwight pointed. He wrote out the receipt and handed Jim back his license. Giving him the change of ownership card, he said, "Don't forget to mail it in. They charge you for the privilege. The State's got to get their pound of flesh."

Jim didn't smile as Dwight handed him the bill of sale.

Dwight kept going. "The Chevy is yours now. Sold as-is. You don't hold me responsible for anything wrong once you drive it off this property, etcetera, etcetera. You know the drill but I have to say it. It's the law. People have trouble with the fine print." He bit twice on the end of the pen like it was a piece of jerky. "We're set. Anything else I can do you for?"

"No." Jim got out of the chair.

"Say," Dwight looked at the photocopy with the license and cash. "You any relation to the Forst Funeral Home people?"

"I'm Jim's cousin. His dad, Virgil, and my dad were brothers. We're the only ones left. Jim, and recently his grandparents and Cousin Nate, are dead." Moisture dampened his neck. Jim hated being dead. He put his wallet back in his pocket and took the keys to his new car. "Got an extra set?"

"Yea, I heard about it. Sorry." Dwight opened a side drawer and got a box. He pawed through it, checking the tags. "Got it," and he handed them over. "License says, James." He squinted as he looked up. "You signed Matthew."

"I'm James Matthew; Cousin Jim was James Robert, after a great-grandfather. People say we looked like twins.

I go by Matt. Don't want to be mistaken for a dead cousin."

Dwight nodded. "Right. I remember. Kids see a movie "Rebel Without a Cause," and they gotta try it out for themselves. There's no more racing in the pit. Police shut it down. Tuff for you, though, losing your family."

"Jim and I weren't close. Understood he was a hothead. Still." Playing on the man's sympathies wouldn't hurt. Jim didn't know if Dwight bought the story or not.

"Are you staying to take over the family business?"

"No. It's closed for good. I'm here to straighten up a few loose ends and be on my way."

"If you need anything, Matt, let me know. I got other good deals sitting on the lot ... in case you decide you want to trade up."

Jim didn't answer. He put the extra set of keys in his pocket.

Dwight thought a moment, "You know, my father taught me it's the details that count." He reached into the pocket of his shirt and handed him a card for a car wash. "First wash is on me. Tell Ike I sent you. He'll take care of you."

"I'll use it." He went out the door, grabbed his bike, popped the lock in the glove box to open the trunk, and pushed it in. With a bit of maneuvering, he closed the trunk lid. Sliding into the driver's seat, he rolled down the window. "See you around," he called to Dwight, who followed him outside.

"See you around." Nodding in a friendly, Idaho way. He put both his hands into his pants pockets.

Jim drove to the edge of the road, looked both ways, gunned it across, hung a left, and headed to the other side of town. Reaching for the car radio, he dialed through the stations until he found something suited to his mood, some hard rock. He hated cry-baby, country-western nonsense. Jim needed to get the business back at hand. He still wasn't having any fun, but at least lying was easy.

Chapter 6

Missy, with luck, didn't have a klutz episode on the bus to and from school the next day. Brandon said hi both morning and afternoon as Missy tried her hardest not to look at him. She squeaked a "Hi" back and was shocked Kaleb didn't say a word about her being a klutz.

Not too long after Missy arrived home from school, Tommy yelled down the hall to her bedroom. "Missy Miss. Julie's here."

"Come on in. I'm in the back." Missy needed a break from working on a history paper.

"You come here." Julie summoned from where she stood at the front of the hall.

Missy pushed her chair back from her desk, stood and headed to the front room. "What's going on?"

Julie looked around. "I'm bored. Let's go for a motorcycle ride."

"Na, don't feel like it."

"What? That's so not you." Julie touched Missy's forehead. "You sick?"

She faked a laugh. "I'm fine." Missy walked out the backdoor to the trampoline and sat.

"You seem a little cranky lately." Julie sat next to Missy.

"Haven't slept much."

"Why?"

Missy stared at the bushes on the side of the fence for a few seconds. "Dreams."

"I remember you saying it the other day. So why do they keep you awake?" She looked at Missy. "Oh, I bet it's romantic dreams of Brandon, eh?"

"Oh my heck, I haven't even met him. I crunched *pop tarts* on his shirt but never got a good look at his face. I look the other way when I get on the bus." Missy knew better. She glanced at Brandon any chance she could get. "Plus, I've been dreaming before he moved here."

"Why are they keeping you up?"

Missy shrugged. "You'd think I was weird." She squinted at Julie, still debating whether to tell her. "I don't want to freak you out."

"I'm sitting here, right? I'm your friend and want to be more of one." Julie fidgeted with a leaf.

"I have precognition dreams at night. Sometimes during the day, I feel a premonition. You know, like something's going to happen."

Julie didn't look surprised at all. "You mean you can tell the future like a card reader or those magic crystal balls?"

"No. I get a feeling of a certain person involved but don't know what will happen. An impression. I can't explain it any better." Missy stared at the bushes again.

"Like the one police show on T.V. where the gal uses sign language dreams of who did what after she knows what the problem is?"

"Yes and no. Here is the weird part. What I think I'm dreaming of turns out to be really happening. I'll wake up and my dream is still happening in real life."

Julie's lips moved around while she thought. "Let's say we're sitting here right now. You fall asleep, dream we're jumping, and you'll wake up jumping?"

"Something like that." Missy didn't mention the backhoe across the street in the field running during the night. She got up and made small jumps. "But I'm wide awake now." Julie joined. They jumped for a few minutes until Julie went home. Missy continued to do knee and butt landings and questioned why she had strange dreams.

Chapter 7

Wednesday, mid-morning, Jim knew it was a waste of time relooking out back in his junky dirt yard digging holes in the ground. He was hungry and was tired of fast food. He grunted and threw the near-empty bag into the garbage can. *If I have to eat one more bite of day-old food, I'm going to get sick.*

A low profile had been easy for Jim to keep, except with Dwight at the car lot. He had a look, a sort of devious, weasel-eyed look, and it didn't sit right with Jim. He had a feeling Dwight might do some research to see if a Mathew James Forst existed.

Jim wished Dwight would forget they'd done any business at all. He didn't want the guy to snoop around. Or did he? Maybe Dwight would be a great helper on the treasure hunt. Jim decided the name fit. When he found the goods, his life would be rich.

Jim looked at the clothes he bought at the thrift store. Black pants, a black long-sleeved shirt, and a black hat. It would keep people away. People tended to be skittish concerning others dressed in all black. He was tired of this place.

He felt "ants in his pants" and had to leave. He knew something was pushing him away from going to the shack and the field. The timing wasn't right. So, his next choice was to go to Sears and buy a fridge. He needed food. He wanted actual food. Scrounging through leftovers of day-old take-out was for the birds.

Driving into the Sears parking lot, he found a space near the door. Jim moseyed in and squinted. Everything was white: the walls, the floor, and the appliances. Overhead were long rods of fluorescent lighting. The glare was ridiculous.

Moving through the appliance section, he noticed black-colored fridges against the wall at the back. He headed over, knowing he wouldn't be waiting long. Business wasn't good enough to let a customer stand around. Jim gave the salesperson three seconds: three, two, one, and bingo. One scurried over to him like a squirrel waiting for a nut to be dropped.

"Hi, I'm Bob. Can I help you?" He clapped his hands together and rubbed them briskly.

"Need a small fridge."

"For your kid going off to college?"

Jim ignored this scenario. "I need a small fridge," he repeated. Bob looked at the larger stainless-steel models lining the wall with a hopeful glance. Jim knew he was thinking about his commission on the big, four-thousand-dollar plus model with six doors and the ice-maker-slash-water-dispenser on the front. Jim turned away from the large models and headed towards the dorm-sized fridges on the back shelf.

Bob nodded and place his hands together as if getting ready to pray. Jim wished he could put permanent glue on the guy's hands so they would stay there. He hated the flapping like a de-headed chicken act. Let him work for the sale. Jim didn't say a word.

The tactic worked. The man collapsed on himself like a deflated balloon. His excitement for a big sale drizzled out the door. "We have a few small models. What we call 'office refrigerators'. I'll show you."

Jim felt like strangling the little twerp as he followed him to another aisle. What a dweeb. A minute later, he found Bob standing next to a white fridge 4 feet tall and 2 feet wide. He demonstrated it by opening the door and pointing out the freezer.

"This is one of the frost-free models."

The fridge was perfect. He didn't want to spend his time chipping out the freezer compartment. Jim peered in. *Big enough for one ice tray and a few other items. It would do.*

"How much?"

"We give new customers 15% off when they open an account." Bob swung his arms back and forth as in hope of a sale improved.

Jim looked at the price ticket: one-hundred and seventy dollars. "I don't want to open an account."

"If we open a new account, you save the twenty-five bucks, even if you don't come back. Henh-henh. Right?"

It must be his idea of Idaho humor. "No, I'm set." Jim fumbled through his snake-skin wallet as he followed Bob to the counter to write up the sale.

"Positive? Twenty-five is twenty-five." Bob raised his eyebrows. "I can get you a dorm-sized microwave for fifty dollars with a new account."

Jim thought. *If I opened the account, I'd save twenty-five dollars and get a microwave, too. But opening an account meant giving information.*

"No, but I think I'll get the microwave. Add it to my bill."

"Your total with tax is," the sales guy punched in the numbers on the register, "two hundred-thirty-two dollars and fifty cents."

Jim opened his wallet and counted out five fifty-dollar bills. Three bogus and two real currencies. He shook as he handed them to Bob. "Here you go."

"Cash, perfect." He rang it up in the register. "Must be hungry, you're shaking."

"Didn't have breakfast." Jim noted Bob didn't bother seeing to see if the bills were good. Fine. The little dweeb counted back seventeen dollars and fifty cents in change.

"Pleasure doing business with you. We'll get Bernie to load the dolly and take the items out to your car. Give me a minute."

"Fine. I'll pull my car up to the loading bay."

"Hey, Bernie," Bob called.

Jim watched Bob walk through the door to the back of the store. He didn't like toadies. He thought it would be fun to run Bobby Boy over with his car. Nice. Some people irked him.

Chapter 8

During lunch, Missy worked on her English paper as Julie sat by her and ate plain lettuce. Julie seemed a little off since Missy told her about her dreams, but Missy dealt with it.

"Have you ever liked someone more than normal?" Missy glanced at Julie.

"What do you mean, more than normal?"

Missy thought for a minute. "How about like at first sight?"

"Oh. You're thinking about Brandon. I'm sure every girl he walks by will fall head over heels for him."

"No. Wrong feeling. This feels different."

"Nope, not yet, or I'm sure I'd understand." Julie took a bite of her salad. "You want to know something strange? I smelled a weird but sweet fragrance when I walked by the boys' bathroom before lunch. It could pass as a type of perfume, not cologne. Too girlish of a smell."

"Sounds like Twist to me. I smelled it once. Sweet in a weird way."

"You've been acting strange saying it's lack of sleep. Are you sure? Are you hiding something from me?"

"What? I haven't been weird. You should know I'm not stupid enough to try anything past a Coke or Pepsi. Caffeine's the limit." Missy gathered her lunch tray and stood. "The bell's about to ring. I'll see you later."

Missy dumped her half-eaten lunch in the trash and put her tray on the counter of the dishwasher's room. She and Julie were good friends, but not quite best friends.

Missy kept her problems to herself and hoped Julie didn't imagine her getting into drugs, but Julie knew she was vulnerable and wanted to be included with the popular kids like Maura and Ally.

***

Jim now had a refrigerator and a microwave, but there was still a lack of food. The next stop was the grocery store. The parking lot was packed and luckily, he found a spot at the end.

Jim made his way back to the produce section with his cart. It must be the end-of-the-week special, so he kept going and squeezed in between a couple of ladies to see if any meat was on sale.

"Excuse me, please," a lady said behind him. Jim turned a tad to his left. He saw a Nampa matron reaching for a small rib-eye steak. She was gussied up wearing a Corduroy pink coat. She glared at an even older Nampa matron who wore a black and white checkered coat. On her head was a little black hat with a feather. Little old

Mrs. Black Hat with a Feather also wanted the same marked-down ribeye. Jim held in a laugh.

He took a step back while Mrs. Corduroy Coat pushed her way in. She gave Jim a flirty, approving glance and smiled a fake smile. She scowled at Mrs. Black Hat with a Feather and with one good pull, commandeering the rib eye steak. "Thank you, young man."

"Thank you for what?" Jim smiled, but Mrs. Corduroy Coat didn't reply, and as she added the steak to her cart, was on to her next conquest. Mrs. Black Hat with a Feather had been defeated. After shoving a few packages of meat around, Mrs. Black Hat shook her head and moved to another spot.

Jim watched both ladies going down the same aisle. There were battles of will to come. He could see a fight over the last box of Striped Shortbread or maybe a can of seasoned bread crumbs. *Oh, stop it*, he said to himself.

After a minute or two, he realized he knew who Mrs. Corduroy Coat was but couldn't recall her name. She had been his math teacher back in high school and taken an extra interest in Jim. It was the only class he didn't have to worry about passing. She had had the hots for him. Now, she was a dumpy lady, and Jim was happy she didn't recognize him. *I feel like talking to her, say any little thing, but can't. I'm dead.*

As his old teacher headed for the egg case, he decided she liked the idea of cutting in and edging someone else out. Jim trailed behind, grabbed a few items as he went, but kept watching Mrs. Corduroy Coat. She pushed her cart to the front of the store and got in line. She never looked back, so it was definite she hadn't recognized him. His luck was holding.

He still watched her when a nice-looking woman came out at the end of the aisle and turned her cart his way. His heart stopped. Violet. Oh, no. Violet. He would have recognized her anywhere and knew she would recognize him. They had too much history together.

I'm ruined if Violet knows I'm alive. He turned his back and scrutinized the cereals. Jim had a hard time not glancing at her. She was still drop-dead gorgeous.

Phew. Jim kept his eyes glued to the shelves as she passed him and kept going. She never turned her head to look, but he thought, *Of course, I'm dead.*

From the corner of his eye, he saw her turn at the end of the aisle. He was safe for the moment, but he had to get out of the store. He still needed food, so he took a chance.

Returning to the meat section, Jim grabbed a package of pork chops and headed in the opposite direction from where he last saw Violet. He caught sight of her taking groceries off the shelves, and he made it his business to go the other way each time. Anytime he saw her, he waited until she looked the other way, crossed to the next aisle and kept going. Shopping had lost its pleasure. The people who were safe were toadies like Bob at Sears, or lazy cheaters like Dwight.

He made it to the checkout line and felt frantic. Violet stood two people ahead of him, one line over. This was not good, but he couldn't stop watching her. She dropped a few coupons and bent over to pick them up, and when she stood, their eyes locked for an instant. Jim turned his back and gave his attention to waiting his turn. He knew she was watching but forced himself not to look back.

"Ma'am," the cashier said. "It's your turn."

Mrs. Mack turned away, unloaded her items from her shopping basket, and dropped her coupons again. Jim saw her hands quiver.

Jim made sure his back was the only view Violet had of him if she looked again. He placed his first item on the grocery belt. Was there any chance she recognized him? His mind raced.

He remembered cuddling with Violet in a blanket under the bleachers at the sports field and kissing her, followed by more arguing and more kissing. *I drove around town with her and showed her off to Virgil, who was not supportive at all.*

Virgil would say, "Those kinds of girls, she's going to dump you. You aint good enough for her."

He had wanted to smash Virgil's head in, but he was right. In the end, she dumped him for a jock.

"Sir," said the cashier and interrupted his thoughts.

"Sorry," Jim replied and finished unloading his groceries onto the belt.

He headed for the door with the grocery bags. Mrs. Mack walked to the opposite side of the parking lot. If she didn't recognize him, no one would. He could do what he came for and get out of this town for good.

Jim got to his car, put the bag on the seat and drove off. It looked like he was still safe, but boy, he was tired of being dead.

***

Mrs. Mack put her groceries in the back of her car out in the parking lot and sat in the driver's seat. A lightning bolt of pain shot through her left eyeball, and she needed to catch her breath. She wasn't prepared for a migraine and a Pepsi would do the trick.

Missy's mom squinted against the painful sunlight, got sunglasses out of her purse, put them on, and hoped it would help until she got home. On auto-drive, she headed for the *Red Steer*.

As she pulled up to the drive-through window, a young girl with dyed orange hair peeked out the window.

Another bolt of pain raced through Mrs. Mack's skull and she grimaced as she ordered the Pepsi. Despite feeling sick, she ordered a large order of tater-tots, too. Maybe her blood sugar had dropped and triggered the migraine.

She parked in the parking lot and turned off the motor. As she sat in the car with her makeshift lunch, something bothered her besides the pain. *What was it? I can't remember,* but it had to be in *Paul's.* All was fine until she was in the cold section looking for ice cream. *Was it the older lady with a funny hat? No.*

Mrs. Mack remembered as she stood in the checkout line and dropped the coupons, picked them up and looked behind her. *It couldn't be. It was like I'd seen a ghost. But, no. No.*

Her head was killing her. Pain expanded behind her eyes and she felt the pressure explode. Mrs. Mack decided she had no time to think of such things. Putting the bag of tater tots aside, she drank a few sips of her drink, and double checked the lid before putting it in the drink holder. She needed to get home and rest.

After three blocks, she pulled over and parked.

Jim. It was Jim. *It couldn't be, but I'd swear on a stack of Bibles, I saw Jim Forts. My Jim. But Jim has been dead for fifteen years.*

Her chest tightened and she rubbed her sternum to see if it would loosen the constriction. *Why did Jim get into my thoughts? Because I saw a guy wearing a dungaree jacket pushing a cart in the supermarket, and I decided it was him?*

He reminded her of Jim. It was a look-a-like with some slight forming wrinkles. As for Jim, he was dead. And the dead don't come back to go shopping at *Paul's.*

A car horn blasted from behind.

Missy's mom waved her arm out the window for the car to go on by, but it stopped beside her instead, and the driver, a guy with long hair, yelled, "Hey, Lady, will you pull over? Your rear end is sticking right out into the road."

He looked at her for an instant, saw the troubled look and relented a little. "You need to watch it, you know." He sped on by.

***

Memories of Violet raced through Jim's mind as he drove back to the funeral home. Violet. Dang. It was her. *Man, I miss her face in my hands and the touch of her lips.*

He remembered the promise ring he gave her. She was going to give it back to him when she told Jim off at the Tractor race. Instead, he saw her throw it into the dirt pit. He was annoyed. Violet dropped him for Ray. An evil, unhappy night and in the end, it was 'for the best,' his parents explained to him.

Jim was aggravated. Was it best for him or his parents? Not long after, they declared him dead. He came close to dying and almost lost his arm. His parents were in trouble making money the way they were. He felt sad his grandpa and grandma died and wished it had been his parents instead. A pair of vipers, those two.

He found himself parked outside the old funeral home. He didn't remember the rest of the drive. *Violet. After all this time, the last good thing in my life was Violet.*

People I once knew figured I'd end up wasted. Dead. It was no skin off my nose when it happened. I was marking time. Jim chuckled. He hadn't expected it. It kind of bubbled up out of him. It was kind of funny. He was dead, so what did it matter? The way he looked at it, no one expected anything good from him in the first place, so why worry? He chuckled again. It was a rotten world, no matter how you looked at it.

Chapter 9

Mrs. Mack lay on the couch in the front room when Missy got home. Her migraine had eased. "Hi Missy, how was school?"

She sat by her mom. "Not good. A week and a half left in school and the teachers are loading us with homework. I think it's stupid."

"It surprises me too. You'd think the teachers wouldn't want to do any extra grading at the end of the school year. How much do you have?"

"Math, English, and History. I hate them all." Missy stood and went to her room. After dinner and homework pushed her patience, Missy couldn't wait to go to bed. She needed to sleep badly.

"Missy Miss," Tommy, her little brother, called down the hall. She yanked up her pajamas bottoms a split second before he barged in the door. "Will you tell me a bedtime story? You haven't for a long time."

Missy didn't like to be mean to Tommy, but she'd want to strangle the ten-year-old. She stared back.

"Please?" He begged.

A loud sigh escaped her lips. "Go get one of the Goosebumps books and I'll tuck you in. Give me a sec."

He smiled and left her room quickly.

Missy went to the bathroom and splashed cold water on her face. It refreshed her gloominess. A story to her brother might clear her mind. She hated being tagged as a klutz. The thought of trying Twist seemed favorable for a second. Wash all feelings and troubles out of your mind. Missy knew better.

Fifteen minutes later, and after Tommy had fallen asleep halfway through her reading him the story, Missy went to tell her parents a final goodnight. Their bedroom door was closed. They never closed their door unless they were wrapping presents or having a serious discussion. No birthdays coming up, and it made Missy curious. She knew eavesdropping wasn't good, but when she heard the word, "tractor" she couldn't resist.

Missy placed her ear to the door and prayed she wouldn't get caught.

"Ray," Missy heard her mom say. "Either something is wrong with my brain or I saw Jim today at the grocery store."

"Jim Forst? He's dead. We saw the accident."

"I know. Everyone has someone who looks like them. But would a look-alike have the same unique color of eyes?"

They moved away from the door and went to the far side of the room. It was the end of Missy's eavesdropping business. *What accident? Who was Jim? What had happened?* Missy wanted to know.

Missy grabbed a school library book out of her backpack and got comfy in her bed. She read three pages before falling asleep still propped up on three pillows.

Windy nights were common in the Spring. Bushes and small trees sat around the Mack's house. To Missy's dismay, the small tree by her window was close enough for the tips of the branches to scratch on her window. The sound was like fingernails on a chalkboard.

The wind picked up and the scratching continued nonstop. Being in the first realm of sleep, Missy dreamed of herself standing in a field. She saw two Native Americans pounding on coffins. She wasn't sure if they tried to wake the dead or celebrate the passing of a sick soul.

The one whom she assumed was the chief looked sad and held out his hand to her. Before knowing what came next, a louder scratch on the window jolted her awake.

Confused, Missy put the book on the floor and adjusted her pillows. She was used to strange dreams, but not with Native Americans. They were a private, spiritual race and kept things sacred.

The wind calmed and the branches left only sporadic scratches. Like hypnotic music, it helped put Missy back to sleep.

Chapter 10

Jim paced the front office of the funeral home and brain-stormed. He'd delayed as long as he could, and knew he needed help from Dwight, who popped into his brain countless times. Either he'd be great or would turn in Jim, his parents, and destroy the entire drug operation. He bit the bullet and drove to the car lot.

The door to the small office was open and a fan blocked the entrance. Either Dwight was hot or was blowing in clean air to get the musty smell out. Jim stood by the fan and saw Dwight half asleep in his chair. "Knock, knock," he said aloud.

Dwight jerked up in his seat. "Oh, hi there, Matt, come on it."

Jim stepped over the fan and sat in the other decrepit chair. "Tired from a busy morning?"

"Thursdays are pretty dead. I stay here in case a customer appears."

Jim felt new sweat in his armpits. He was nervous to ask Dwight for help. "You said you had other areas to help me out in, am I right?"

Dwight got excited like a kid getting a bike for Christmas. "You bet. What do you need?"

"Fake I.D., untraceable cell phone, and an up-to-date license plate or one of your dealer's plates." He thumped the desk with his fist.

"I knew it. I knew it from the start. You're Jim. You didn't die after all." Dwight got up and got two beers from his fridge. "Or was it a fake you in the tractor, a look-alike?"

Jim accepted the drink and popped the tab. "It was me. The dirt was soft enough to swallow and cushion my whole body except the shoulder. It took the brunt and got reconstructed."

"Why did you play dead?"

"My parents thought it best to have their delivery boy," he pointed to himself, "be nonexistent." Jim gulped half the can.

Dwight grabbed keys off the wall and took a dealer's plate out of a file box. "I'll drive you to Boise in style. There's a pawn shop close to Garden City that will cover all the above on your list."

He led Jim to an older Mercedes Benz with leather seats. "Anything else I can help you with?"

On the ride to Boise, Jim told Dwight his list from A to Z. Dwight agreed to help Jim with the treasure hunt and to be an undead delivery boy.

***

"Missy hates homework," Missy yelled, crumpled her latest rough draft into a ball, and tossed it on the floor. She thought better of it, picked it up, and flattened it out. Nope. Mrs. Buckner would not accept a wrinkled mess. Missy had written it double-spaced on Wide Elementary school notebook paper, and it was still only two pages long. The assignment was yesterday's lunch garbage as far as she was concerned. And to think the teacher wanted them to write and not use the computer. So, old school.

"Mom," she said as she walked into the kitchen.

"Done screaming?"

She forced a smile. "For the moment."

Missy's mom grabbed the last clean plate out of the dishwasher and turned to face her. "Do you have a problem?"

"Ally and I have an English paper due tomorrow. Can I run to her place after dinner so we can finish it?" She rested her elbows on the counter.

"On a school night? I thought you finished your paper."

Missy held up the wrinkled wreck. "I did, but it's not long enough. Ally might help me add more details. I won't stay there long; 8:30 at the latest." She twirled a pen resting on the counter.

Mom turned back to the dishwasher and added a couple of glasses to the rack. "You can go after dinner, but you need to finish loading the dishwasher first."

The pen Missy twirled flew off the counter and hit her mom's arm. Mrs. Mack narrowed her eyes and grinned.

"K, and thanks."

The clop of Tommy's cowboy boots echoed on the linoleum as he came galloping into the kitchen. His cowboy hat fell over his eyes and he tipped his head back as he looked up at his sister.

"Whoa there, cowboy. Where are you going dressed all up?" Mrs. Mack patted her son on his head.

Missy leaned back on the counter. "Why the getup?"

"Going into town, pard'ner?" Their mom played along with Tommy.

"Our class is a-going on a field trip tomorrow to the Stampede."

"Snake River Stampede?" Missy quenched her nose. "But it doesn't start for a couple months."

"I know. They're gonna teach us how the Stampede works, and we get to see bulls and bucking horses." He galloped around the kitchen and came back to the counter.

"Are you going to learn how to rope a cow while sitting on a horse?" Missy pretended to swing a rope.

"Of course not. But we are gonna watch them practice doing it." Tommy smiled and galloped out of the kitchen.

"Whatever," Missy said.

Mrs. Mack looked at her soon-to-be fifteen-year-old daughter. "I notice a change in your attitude and looks. I see my old self in you on the tomboy side."

"Once a tomboy, always a tomboy."

She hugged her daughter. "And be a little nicer to your brother. And by the way, you wanted to see how they prepared for the Stampede at his age. Now, let's set the table and eat."

Her mom reminded missy to finish loading the dishwasher before she could leave. She grabbed her backpack, hopped on the bicycle, and peddled to Ally's. As she lowered the kickstand on Ally's driveway, the front door opened.

"Where's your dirt bike?" she asked.

"Needs gas," Missy replied.

Ally slanted her head a little to the side in disbelief. "Come in. My mom pulled another batch of chocolate chip cookies out of the oven. And I got another surprise." Her face lit up with a big smile.

"Your mom's always making nifty stuff." Missy followed Ally into the kitchen. She took the folder with her homework assignment from the backpack as Ally's mom entered, holding a plate of cookies.

"Hi, Melissa, how are you doing?

"Great. Mmmm, cookies." she smiled.

"Wait until they cool. Help yourself to the milk. It's in the fridge," Ally's mom turned to Ally. "Your dad and I have paperwork to finish. We'll be downstairs in the office if you need anything." She left the kitchen.

When the coast was clear, Missy slumped in the chair across the table from Ally. "Have you chosen a topic yet?"

"Yep. My topic is how to make my mom's famous chocolate chip cookies." Ally pointed to the plate on the counter. "I love the smell of melting chocolate."

"Seems a little too easy, don't you think?"

Ally handed her a cookie. Missy took a small bite off the crispy edge.

"I thought it was a good topic to write about. It's two pages." She handed them to Missy, "Thirsty?"

"Yes."

Ally got a bottle of milk from the refrigerator and poured them both a cup.

Missy swallowed a big gulp. The taste was heaven with the cookie in her mouth. She took another cookie and was ready for a bite when she realized Ally's handwriting was large with extra spaces between the words. "Buckner said not big and sloppy. You're wasted."

Missy nibbled around the edge of the cookie and went toward the middle for a big bite. "Hot, hot," she gasped and took a big gulp of milk. The swallow of milk ran through the hot cookie in her mouth and it loosened a chocolate-coated flood down her throat.

"You're choking?"

She shook her head no and massaged her throat to help the cookie down. Breathing through her nose, she kept stroking. After a few swallows, the last lump of cookie unclogged and sailed into her stomach. "Phew. Y-y-yeah. But man, those cookies taste superb." Missy wiped her mouth with the back of her hand. "My paper isn't long, either. Here. Read it. Help me add more details."

"What's your topic?"

"My topic is 'A Place of Interest'."

"Well?" Ally shrugged.

"Well, what?"

"What's your place of interest?"

"Read it. You'll see."

"I don't want to. Tell me what it is."

"Fine, it's the pit and the tree ditch."

"Are you kidding me?"

"Nope." Missy tapped the two wrinkled pages on the table to make the edges even. "Fine, I'll read it to you. Have another cookie." She hoped Alley choked, too. She let go of the thought and felt bad for thinking about it.

Ally grabbed two more cookies, placed one on Missy's napkin, and sat across from her. "Go ahead, but don't count on me for any info. I can't stand the pit and the ditch."

Missy cleared her throat and read:

"There are two places I like to go. First, there's a vast sage brush field across from the subdivision where I live. A wide irrigation ditch runs through the center. I like to walk along the ditch.

"Not too far down the path sits a large old oak tree. The trunk is so big you can't wrap your arms around it. One branch is nice and fat and hangs eight feet off the ground. The branch has a thick rope tied to it and dangles over the water.

"The ditch is as wide as it is deep as I am tall. During the summer, we swing on the rope and drop into the ditch. We call it the tree ditch.

"On the other side of the field facing north from the ditch sits an old gravel pit we call the pit.

It's the size of a football field and deep. Since the Bowman's Rocks and Gravel *no longer use it as a pit, they have turned it into a junkyard. People throw trash in there such as old furniture, books, and magazines. There's a beat-up spring mattress by an oak tree at the bottom. My dad and his friends did dangerous things there when they were in high school. He, along with several others, raced their motorcycles in the pit. The oddest thing in there is a big, old rusty tractor."*

"A tractor is in the pit?" a voice asked behind Missy.

Missy watched Ally who looked behind her with a flirty grin. She turned around, and there stood Kaleb and Brandon.

"It's not polite to interrupt, Brandon," said Ally with a half-grin.

"No sense hanging out here," Kaleb grabbed a handful of cookies and turned around. "I'll fill yah in. Let's go to my room." Off they strutted down the hall.

"Surprise," Ally said.

Missy dropped her forehead into her hands. *I can't believe I didn't see them.* "Ooh. How long were they standing there? I'm so embarrassed." She closed her eyes.

"At the beginning of your story." Ally laughed. "Your face is red."

Missy sat and touched her cheeks, feeling the heat.

"It's fading now."

"Nice to know."

"Your story's good so far."

"Until I was interrupted."

"I think you've got it covered." Ally said.

She glanced at the clock. 8:40 p.m. "Crap, got to go. Told my mom I'd be back by 8:30." Missy shoved her papers in her backpack. "Thanks for the cookies. See you tomorrow."

"Bye."

Missy went out the front door to her bike. She kicked up the kickstand and swung her leg over the seat. Missy felt someone watching her. She looked up at Ally's house and saw Brandon leaning halfway out Kaleb's bedroom window. He smiled and waved. She hopped on and marathon-peddled home.

Chapter 11

Missy and Ally sat in their usual back seats in third period. Mrs. Buckner had the students pass their reports to the front desk in each row. "Can anyone tell me what you learned about this assignment?"

No one raised their hands.

"Are you telling me with this assignment most of you googled the topic and wrote it down? That's plagiarism, and I'll know when I read your paper." Missy glanced around the classroom and saw some students show guilt in their expressions.

"I want you to rewrite your story during class to be safe. Not exact words, but summarize what you wrote the best you can." Mrs. Buckner sat. She kept her eyes on her students during the rest of the class time to make sure they were writing.

Missy chuckled. "How are you going to summarize your mom's recipe?"

Ally shrugged.

Missy watched her for a few seconds and wrote a summary of her description of the pit and tree ditch. Two paragraphs later, she was done.

After a couple more minutes, Ally showed Missy her paper. It was a hand drawn picture of the cookie and the essential ingredients to make it.

The afternoon bus ride home gave Missy more mixed feelings. She ended up sitting behind Brandon and Kaleb. She pretended they weren't in front of her.

"So happy it's Friday," Julie said.

"I'm not. Mr. Spoon gave us math homework. Said weekends were a waste of time. Homework added character to our well-being. Give me a break. I hate math," Missy whined.

Brandon turned around. "I can help. What is it?"

Missy rolled her eyes. *Great, now I look stupid to the cute guy.* "Algebra." She glanced at Julie with a questioning look. Julie smiled. Missy looked back at Brandon, "I'll survive, but thank you." He nodded and went back to talk with Kaleb.

Missy whispered to Julie. "I can't believe he offered to help me."

"I can. He likes you."

"Ha. More like he feels sorry for me." The bus stopped for Missy to get off. She exchanged goodbyes with her girlfriends. If Brandon said goodbye, Missy didn't hear it, or blocked it out.

***

Mrs. Mack sat in her usual place on the couch in the front room when Missy got home. She still had a slight migraine from her encounter with the Jim look-alike at the grocery store the day before. "Hi Missy, how was school?"

"Grunt. Good 'ol Mr. Spoon gave us math homework. He showed us an easier method to solve the problems instead of the traditional one. I hate it."

Missy's mom put her book down. "What do you mean new skills in math? Nothing can be better than the original."

"Not what Mr. Spoon said. The school district passed a new way for grade school students to pick up on math better. I think it's dumb."

"Your dad is an accountant, so I'm sure if you have any problems, he can help you." Missy's mom took a drink of her Pepsi, noting it needed more ice. She stood up.

"I don't even think Dad could understand the new math version. Utterly stupid." Missy followed her mom to the kitchen.

"Are you going to finish your homework now?"

"No. My brain needs a break. I'm going to ride my motorcycle around the block a few times." Missy walked to her bedroom and tossed her backpack on her bed. She put on her sweats and a T-shirt and made sure her rubber band was tight on her ponytail before she went outside to her motorcycle.

Missy rode around the block once and looked at Brandon's house as she passed it. It sat on the corner, angled across the street from Maura's. There was a small fruit field across from Maura's house.

Missy had a temptation to stop and see if he was home, maybe ask him about the new way of doing math.

Ha, I'd rather sniff or smoke Twist first. She didn't stop, and ended her ride at the tree ditch. She parked her bike, sat on the ground, and leaned against the tree.

The irrigation water was back in force, and soon they would have the summer fun of swinging on the rope to take the plunge.

Missy's parents raised her standards of not trying to smoke, drink, take drugs, or get carried away with boys. Missy knew some of her friends did all the above and seemed happy. She thought what if she tried doing one or two of the BAD stuff and see how she felt. Would it be worth it or better off being a Plain Jane with a boring life?

A peaceful quiet filled Missy as she viewed the neighborhood, the field, the dirt pit, and the shack down the dirt path towards the lake. She'd never been to the shack but knew the town rumored it to be haunted.

Several minutes passed and the sun faded away to the other side of the world. With a few clouds waving goodnight in the sky, it left colorful reflections on the lake. Missy felt a little uncomfortable and knew it was time to go home.

***

The two days' work in Boise got Jim's list of to-dos done including a fake license plate on his car. He drove to the shack. It was getting dark enough not to draw attention.

As he got closer to the turn off, he saw dust on the path. *Small field twister?* No, a girl had stopped at the edge of the road on the dirt path. Jim passed by. *What was she doing on the path? Is the shack a new hangout for teens?* He hoped not.

Jim turned on Ginger Lane, drove a hundred yards, and turned right at the far side of the field on the dirt road. He saw the backhoe under a small carport beside some trees. It still appeared drivable, though it was dirty and a little rusty. He parked close by the carport and walked to the shack.

To his surprise, though the sun was nearly set, he didn't see footsteps by the shack's door. To Jim, it had been ignored and not vandalized. The wind and weather could erase any marks in the dirt, but it looked undisturbed.

The door opened to a dark, musty room. In the corner was a small wooden desk and an old rocking chair. In the opposite corner was a cot covered in dust. Jim's grandparents were friends with Darius, the original owner of the fields on each side of the irrigation ditch. After Darius died thirty-some years ago, in his will, he gave ownership to Jim's parents of the one field they used. Darius gave the other field by the dirt pit to his son who didn't even live in Nampa or Idaho.

Jim knew the night was wasted and walked to the backhoe to see if he could get it to start. He lifted the floor mat on the driver's side and found the key. Not the best way to store a key, but the only place not to forget where it was. Pumping the choke a few times, the engine coughed and started.

Jim yahooed. "Something worked out on the first try." He checked the gages and knew he'd have to add oil and get a large gas tank.

Chapter 12

The field, shack, and backhoe were a mystery to Missy, but it only interrupted her life when the owners drove it at night. It crossed Missy's mind no one should use a backhoe on an empty field. There were no seeds to plant and grow, but it made night runs in the field.

Missy adjusted positions in her bed and continued to think about the backhoe, and as she fell asleep, her mind made its own story for her to dream.

Mr. Spoon, who never smiled, grinned as the students sat. Not a good sign. They waited. Mr. Spoon was famous for his surprise quizzes.

He looked around the class and his eyes settled on Missy. She could feel the fear building inside her and she had goosebumps on her arms. Any day now Mr. Spoon will grow devil horns and breathe fire, she mused.

"You," he said pointing at Missy. "Let me see your homework." He marched to her desk. "Did you do it? I know you stink in math. Why do you bother? I'm waiting." He held out his hand.

"Uh, yes. I got it. It's right here." She shuffled around in her backpack until she found the worksheets and handed them over.

He rolled the papers and snapped them against his pants leg. He went back to his desk, unrolled the homework and flipped through the pages. He laughed. "You call this completed homework?" Mr. Spoon stepped over to the whiteboard, grabbed a dry erase marker and wrote. Each letter screeched as he wrote. The class watched the board. "Melissa is Dumb at Math."

"Do you have your math book?" he yelled.

Missy realized she'd left it in her locker. "N-nooo. I, I forgot it," she squeaked, looked around the classroom, and saw the other students stare back at her in shock.

"Go to your locker and get it now." He eyed Missy with his devil look and smirked. "I want you to show the students how to do my version of pre-algebra." Mr. Spoon thrust a finger toward the door. "Go."

Her chin touched her chest as she left the classroom. The door shut behind her. Missy would never step inside a math class again if she didn't have to. Should she skip out? No, he'd find her and give her evil looks with his undead zombie eyes. He'd chase her, like a hound dog chasing a criminal. He had her scent. Missy shuddered.

She squinted to find her locker. It was dark. Too dark. Something didn't seem right but she had no time to waste. Missy reached her locker. It was the easiest one to recognize, it had the most scratches on it.

Brrr. Brbrbr. Thwok.

She froze. Not the tractor. Thwok. "M-e-l-i-s-s-a. M-e-l-i-s-s-a," a voice called.

Brrr Brbrbrbr Thwok. Brrr Brbrbr. The tractor rumbled over weeds and rocks.

"Who's out there?" Missy screeched and leaned against the lockers. Heat rose up her back. Her shirt soaked from the sweat and she fanned herself with her hands. Small stabs of nail tips crawled up her back like spiders. She spun around. There was a big hole where her locker should have been. Flames shot out of it. Horrible, ugly, razor like fingers reached to grab her.

Missy screamed and ran up the school's hall to the main entrance of the school.

Brrr, Brbrbr Thwok. Brrr, Brbrbr. The tractor groaned.

Boom. Screech.

"My ears!" She covered them with her hands and turned in a circle to find a place to escape.

Thud. Crack.

She stopped turning and saw the glass doors at the end of the hallway.

Crack. Thud.

Big black wheels smashed through and shattered the doors. Dust, wood, and glass splinters flew in all directions. Missy ducked as a glass shard flew toward her and crashed on the linoleum floor, breaking into a million pieces.

Brrrr Brbrbr.

The big, black, rusty old farm tractor was still coming, and Mr. Spoon was driving it. "I'll get you, Melissa. Ha-ha-ha-ha. I will teach you for not doing your homework, ha-ha-ha. I'll teach you to not leave your math book in your locker, ha-ha-ha."

She turned and ran down the hall as the tractor at her heels got closer and closer. I'm fast, I can make it. I can make it. Puff, puff. Missy tripped and landed flat on her face.

Buzz, Buzz. She reached out and tried to stifle the noise.

Bang. She felt the jolt.

Buzz, Buzz, Buzz.

Throbbing pain exploded in Missy's hand from hitting the clock. She sat up, hoping she wouldn't pass out. The alarm clock buzzed on the floor and almost put her entire weight on it as she stood. She'd pick it up later. Advil called Missy's name and she went to the bathroom to get it.

If Mr. Spoon continued to give her nightmares, she was going to switch teachers for the last week of school.

Chapter 13

Missy kept busy on Saturday to keep her mind off her math homework. She went over to Julie Brown's house and played on her family's foosball table.

Julie inspected Missy and handed her the foosball ball to start the game. "You look a little pale."

Missy put the ball in the slot and pushed it. "Something weird's going to happen. I don't know what, but can feel it."

Julie hit the ball to the side. Missy missed it and Julie retrieved it with her upper foosball bar players and made a goal. "You think something bad will happen?" She got the ball and put it in the slot.

"I had a dream last night about Mr. Spoon chasing me on the old rusty tractor in the pit. He told me to give up on math." She tried to block the ball from Julie but wasn't paying close attention. Julie got another score.

"And the other night when I was at the Tree Ditch thinking, I started getting an uneasy feeling. Not bad, but kind of unnatural." Missy hit the ball backward and got Julie another score.

Julie stopped playing and looked at Missy. "You mean like a ghost was close by? Weird things happen at night." She walked over to the couch and sat. Missy followed.

"I can't hide it any longer, Julie. My mind's going crazy."

"Hide what?"

"For years, a backhoe has been driving around the field across the street. Then it stopped. But it's happening again. I see it from my window. The backhoe doesn't scare me, but whoever's driving it or what they're looking or digging for isn't right. I can feel it."

Julie adjusted her position on the couch. "I've never heard the backhoe noise but read in the paper some time ago it was disturbing neighbors as night. They think the funeral home owners are using it as you would say, 'A storage place'.

Missy rolled her eyes. "What would they be storing in the ground? Unknown dead bodies? The funeral home is downtown. They should stack them on top of each other in their garage."

"Gross." Julie got up and went to her family's old quarter slot machine with a pull handle and a bowl full of quarters sat by it. Her parents' rules were, you didn't keep the money you won, of course, but it was fun to see how much you could win with each run. "Let's see who the next millionaire is."

Missy joined, glad for the distraction, and went home an hour later.

Later in the day, Missy did retreat to the tree ditch to clear her mind and to see if she felt the uneasy feeling again. Plus, she procrastinated to do her math. No bad feelings hit her.

She promised Tommy to watch Saturday Night Fright with him before the news came on at 10:00 pm. The shows were old, based back in the 1970s, so they weren't scary and didn't bother Tommy at all.

During the night, Tommy had a nightmare and woke Missy up. "Missy, are you awake?"

She forced her eyes open. "What? Go to bed. I'm sleeping."

"You are not," Tommy sat on the side of the bed.

Missy scooted closer to the wall. "Yes, I am. Go back to bed and try or go tell mom."

"I didn't want to wake her up."

"I'm not your mom and don't want to be woken up either." Missy wasn't in the mood for being pleasant, but it came naturally. "The show gave you nightmares?"

Tommy got his pillow off the floor, and Missy didn't see it beforehand. "Can I sleep with you?"

"Did you have a bad dream?"

"I can't remember."

"Fine, sleep on the floor and use my quilt." Missy hoped Tommy didn't inherit her ability to foreshadow.

***

Midafternoon on Sunday, Missy forced herself to her desk and opened the math book. It almost scared her a hand would jump out and grab her, but knew it wouldn't happen. *Or could it happen? I'm sure if I sniffed some Twist it would. It would also help me face math and Mr. Spoon.*

Missy's left arm tingled from the weight of her head as she doodled on the paper with shapes, not numbers.

"Melissa," Mom yelled.

"What?" She jerked up in a sitting position.

Maura entered Missy's room. "Missy, girl, are you still working on math? I told myself to forget his new problem-solving creation. I did it the usual way."

"Either way, I'm so not a math person." Missy looked at her. Not a good thing to say. It was too good an opening for Maura to pass up, but she shrugged. "You bored?"

"A little. We're done with school in five days and I have a sweet tooth."

"A sweet tooth? I have a sour one. Math." Missy twirled her pencil.

Maura walked over and poked a finger at the worksheet. "You need a break." She flipped the pencil out of Missy's hand, across the room, and landed on her bed. She smiled. "I told your mom we're going out for ice cream and my mom volunteered to take us."

Why was Maura being friendly? Should I be suspicious? Missy needed a break. She followed her out the front door. Maura's mom, Linda Derringer, waited for them in the driveway.

"Hop in," They piled into the back seat of the car.

"Hi, Missy." Maura's mom looked at her in the rearview mirror.

"Hi. You're kidnapping me. What gives?"

Maura did her spiraling thing with her hair. "How about Dairy King for a parfait Sound good?"

"Of course. But why?"

"Just because."

Good enough for me, Missy thought. The math problems would be waiting for her when she got back, but at least now she wouldn't have to think about it.

Linda said, "School's almost out and I think it deserves a reward."

Missy smiled. "Ah gee, thanks."

The invitation was Maura's mom's idea. She seemed to have a soft spot in her heart for Missy, and she could stand a little spoiling right now from any direction.

They got to Dairy King and went in.

"Maura, do you think they'll give us extra peanuts? Oomph!" Missy hadn't been looking where she was going and banged hard into someone. Taking a step back she lost her balance. A pair of hands grabbed her arms to keep her from kissing the floor.

Missy turned and looked up and saw Brandon. "Uh. oh, sorry." Missy stuttered. "How many times have I run into you? I guess this must be a record," she said with a weak smile

Brandon steadied her before letting her go. "No prob. Ankle hurt?"

"No. Uh, but thank you and nice catch." *What a crappy thing to say. Me and my blabbering mouth.* Missy turned and followed Maura and her mom to a booth. "Did you know he was going to be here?"

"No," Maura said.

Her eyes narrowed.

"I promise I didn't. It was Mom's idea to come."

She could be telling the truth. Missy looked back at the door and saw Brandon leaving. He turned, made eye contact, and grinned.

She turned back around and Maura looked pleased, like she approved. *Will I ever figure Maura out?* She wondered.

"Brandon's a nice-looking kid and the family appears to be nice," Linda said. "I ran into his mother, Rita Miller, at the grocery store the other day. Says she likes the neighborhood."

"For now," Maura muttered.

Maura's mom looked at Missy for info, but she only shrugged. She didn't know what Maura was implying. Also, Missy made it a rule to stay out of other families' mother-daughter conversations.

The clerk called their number. Linda retrieved the order of Peanut Buster Parfaits with a bowl of extra peanuts on the side.

"Heaven is what I call this," Missy said as she dumped a spoonful of nuts on top of her parfait and shoveled a big bite into her mouth, "An' whiff th' nuts," she mumbled as she chewed and swallowed, "Peanut Busters are known to provide the protein and iron for running fast and jumping high." Missy said. She sounded like an advertisement.

They laughed.

They dropped Missy home from Dairy King at 8 p.m. and she went straight to her room. At nine Missy's math assignment was done. It was the best she could do. She knew her Dad was watching T.V. and Tommy was asleep.

Thanks for the small miracle. He'll be out of my hair tonight. Missy's mom was reading in the front room.

"Mom?" Missy sat by her on the couch.

Mrs. Mack marked the page and placed her book on the end table. "Yes, dear?"

"Um." Missy exhaled.

"Um, what?"

"I don't know."

She placed her hand on Missy's back. It felt good. "Did you have a spat with Maura?"

"No." Missy rested her chin in her hand, her elbow on her knee. "See, Maura, Julie, and Ally are popular. And I'm, I'm…" Missy waved her hand around. "I'm not popular. But, there's this boy, I don't know him. I mean I've seen him a couple of times. He's being nice, like he's glad to see me." Missy pulled a face and slumped against the pillows. She'd ran out of steam.

"You like a boy? Something wrong?"

"I don't know," shrugging. "Nothing, I guess. But, I mean, I've never had a boyfriend, and if it's true this kid, Brandon, likes me, and I think he might. I don't have what I'm saying."

Why can't I talk and get it out? She turned and looked at her mom. "I want to stand out but not be a fake. Make sense?

Mom's face went still, but Missy could almost read her thoughts about popularity or lack of it.

"So, you've run into this boy. It's a start. What you need to remember, if I read this right, a true friend will stick by you no matter what. Even if they like something you have and they don't, like a boyfriend. If you lose one of your friends because of a boy, she wasn't a real friend."

Mom scooted to the edge of the couch. "A good night's sleep will often help cure the worries." She took Missy's hand and pulled her into a hug.

"Thanks, Mom. I feel better."

"Nighty-night."

"Good night, Mom." She passed the T.V. room, "Night, Dad." He nodded. She continued to her room and climbed into bed. She was ready for a good night sleep. Would she have one?

Chapter 14

Dwight sat on the couch with Jim at the funeral home. Pointing at the map he said, "So you're telling me where each X is on the map is where a coffin is buried, right?"

"Right, and hopefully my grandparents buried a huge supply of Twist and the ingredients for making it." Jim took a drink of generic beer. "We need to plan to dig on a cloudy night. Should have luck with some fog, too, being by the lake."

Dwight followed suit by taking a drink. "I'll let you do the digging but will help go through the treasure when you uncover it. I can wait in the shack or you can call me when you're done."

"Will do, and see you later."

Dwight left to open his car lot.

Jim looked at the map again. He moved to the chair and rested his feet on the desk. He still wasn't a hundred percent sure he wanted Dwight to help him out all the way. "Now where did you old buzzards hide the gear? Hmm? What casket?"

The map of the field was accurate, with the measurements notated. It included the shack, situated 50 feet from the open parking space in a field, where the backhoe sat. He knew his grandparents had stored other things in caskets. They, too, were marked on the map, near the parking space.

Jim's grandparents had been savvy, or shady. One of the caskets contained English Royal antiques they'd taken in trade for fake cash, knowing the items would be a good investment, worth a small fortune in a future trade. They were marked as being twenty feet to the left of the shack. *Nice little bonus.* He smirked. They had been safe trading when the hearse was running, but he was not sure how much longer their safety would last. His parents did things more old fashion like his grandparents. Computer work was too much for them.

The map indicated a couple of places he hadn't known existed. "What did they want me to do? Dig up the whole dang field?"

Jim slid his feet off the desk and onto the ground floor. Standing up, he slammed the map on the desk, turned, and hammered his fists on it.

He looked up to the ceiling as if his grandparents were floating above. "I've looked in this so-called building inside and out including the trashed trailer and hearse. Where did you put the secret recipe? Where? I'm tired of looking and don't want to dig the whole place up." He grabbed the chair and threw it across the floor. There were a lot of goodies out there. He needed them. "I'm ready to dig up their graves and shake their skeletons until they tell me."

Bang. Bang. Bang.

Jim landed blow after blow on the wall. "Walls have to be good for something besides holding up the ceiling," he barked, and gave the wall one more solid whack for good measure.

Pounding something solid helped ease his frustration. He stopped, took a deep breath and snatched the map. Time to find the first casket.

Not wanting to take the time to make a meal, Jim went to Red Steer. As he drove in the drive-through, he thought, *another place with enjoyable memories. This one was eating cheeseburgers and playing pinball. Which one was it? Oh yea, Centipede. Violet always had the highest score when she played. Violet.* He swallowed hard.

You know you're a sucker for thinking of her. She dumped you, remember?

He scanned the menu. It didn't look any different. Familiar stains dotted its surface. Nice to know certain things never change.

"Place your order when you're ready," a familiar voice said. It was Ruth. The cute-looking redhead.

"Number three with cheese and a large Cherry Pepsi."

"The total is $6.55. Pull up, please."

Jim grabbed a ten-dollar bill out of his wallet as he drove up to the window. He had his arm out holding the money.

"Would you like fry sauce?" she took the ten and noticed it was Jim. "Hi." Her smile brightened.

"Hi, and yes."

"Yes?" She crinkled her face.

"Fry sauce."

"Got it." She grabbed a handful of small containers of the sauce and dropped them in the take-out bag. "This ought to hold you for a while." Handing him his change and the order, she looked behind his car. No other customers were waiting.

"Two jobs?"

"Yeah. But this one is sporadic. I come in when I'm needed. But I'm free most evenings." She winked at Jim.

Jim smiled. "Good for you." Jim started to leave but stopped. "Ruth, is there still the Centipede game inside?"

"Amazingly yes, along with an auto race game."

He nodded and drove away, feeling stupid for asking a silly question. He headed out to the shack. Jim wondered if Violet's name was still on the top ten scores. *Might have to go in sometime and look.* But there was Ruth. If he kept running into the redhead, it was going to ruin his concentration.

Jim arrived at the shack and parked. His goal was to organize the map and put a mark at each spot so he knew where to dig with the backhoe at night.

Jim got ecstatic. A heavy blanket of clouds sat low on Nampa, combined with light fog on the field. He yearned to dig instead of marking where to search. But it all depended on the time it took to dig and the cooperation of Mother Nature. Maybe she would be nice to him tonight and not clear the fog and clouds.

He swallowed his excitement and marked the spots on the map as he ate instead. It didn't take too long with his energy from a few sniffs of Twist as well.

Chapter 15

Math class ended and it was lunch time at school. Missy rested her head on her folded arms at the table. Maura, Julie, and Ally were yapping. There was a certain harmony to it. She couldn't make out the words, except for a random comment about a cute boy, but the gentle buzz of the conversation soothed her fractured psyche.

"His hair looks so soft."

Missy couldn't tell who whispered the words.

"I'd love to run my fingers through…"

The words drifted off as Missy snoozed.

Maura patted Missy's back. "You're snoring."

She sat up, still looking groggy. "No. No, I wasn't."

"Yes, you were," Julie said. "But you are awake now. Right?"

"Homework, Mr. Spoon," she mumbled.

"Why are you so tired?" Maura asked.

"Mr. Spoon?" Ally gave a confused look.

"He… never mind."

Maura blurted, "You did turn in the math assignment?"

"Yes."

"You were saying what did Mr. Spoon do?" Ally asked.

"Forget it." Missy flapped her hand.

Julie got it. "Change of subject. Is anyone here thinking of Brandon?"

"No," Missy said.

"I think you were dreaming of B-B-B-Braaandon," Maura decided.

"Not even close."

Maura smirked.

"I need more sleep," Missy said.

She made it through the last two classes without drifting off to sleep. When school was out and with a strange occurrence, Missy ended up sitting by Brandon on the bus.

"Did the teachers give you lots of homework?" Brandon's shoulder nudged Missy's once.

She quickly glanced at Brandon and glued her eyes on her backpack. "Enough to drive me crazy."

"Totally understand."

Missy couldn't think of anything else to say, so she kept quiet. Brandon got the hint and did the same.

After night chores were done and last minute homework make-ups done, Missy sat on the couch with her journal. She hadn't written in it for a while.

Dear Journal,

I've been bad at writing, but yah know, with homework, gymnastics, track, and school almost out, I'm dead as a crumbled up stick you'd find in the pit. Scared, scraped up knees and left-over bruises included.

My friendship with Ally, Maura, and Julie is okay, I guess. They talk about Brandon half the time and they wonder if one of us will be lucky enough to be his girlfriend. The odds favored Ally; he's great friends with Kaleb and is over at their house a lot.

I'm not getting much sleep because of the nightmares. They're happening more often. The tractor and…

"You dream of big tractors squishing cars and people, too?" Tommy was excited to know.

"Ah!" Missy screamed and slammed her journal shut. "You butthead. I don't come and read your journal, do I?" Missy grabbed his nose hard.

"Ow. Let go!" Tommy yelled and tried to push her hand away.

"You stop reading what I'm writing. Do you hear me?" She squeezed his nose tighter. When she let go, it left a red mark.

He touched his nose. "I didn't do anything. You're mean." He slapped her head and stomped to his room.

"Aargh. Tommy." Missy had gone too far and knew it. "Tommy, get back here." His bedroom door slammed. She didn't want to get up, but knew she better and went to Tommy's room. She knocked on his door.

"Stay away," he yelled.

She ignored his command, opened the door, and sat next to Tommy on his bed. He rubbed his nose again.

"Go away," he snapped.

"I'm sorry, li'l bro. You scared me. Come here. Let me see it." He turned and gave her a sad look. "Hmm. It isn't red anymore."

"It still hurts."

"Not after this." Missy Eskimo kissed his face and made him laugh. "Sorry. Look, my journal. It's private. No one can see it. You understand?"

He nodded. She took hold of his head and gave his nose another nuzzle. "Will Eskimo kisses pass?" He nodded again.

"I'm getting a little hungry. Might have to make me a sardine sandwich." He lay down and smiled as Missy rolled him up in his blanket. Nice and secure.

"Night."

"Good night, Tomster." She closed the door. *I have no idea how he can dream about tractors like me unless he's seen the backhoe and thinks it's a tractor? At this moment, I don't want to worry about it.*

Strange thoughts crossed Missy's mind as she fell asleep. A tractor drove around in the field making design pictures in the dirt. It dug in spots and came up with rubber arms stretching out.

The tractor dug so deep, it woke Missy up. She thought it was an earthquake as her bed had a slight vibration. Or maybe it was rubbery arms crawling out of the grave in the field? She dozed back to sleep and heard a noise.

Brrr brbrbr thwok. Brrr brbrbr thwok. "Melissa." *Brrr brbrbr thwok.*

She jolted up and gasped for air. Through her bedroom window, fog filled her eyes and caused her body to twitch.

Please no.

A flicker of light brightened a section through the fog, rested on the field, and faded. *The backhoe?*

Maybe Julie was right about the funeral home owners storing stuff in the field. Missy never understood why a farmer would drive around his field in the middle of the night.

She knelt on her bed, scrunched her nose against the window and looked across the street. Her eyes weren't playing tricks on her. Even in the fog, she saw the backhoe, its motor growling in the shimmering moonlight. Its two prominent headlights faded as it circled left at the bottom of the field. She got out of bed and went to the front room, parting the drapes and peering through the large picture window.

It could have been a car going down Ginger Lane. Narrow headlights appeared once more. To Missy, it seemed more like eyes haunting her. She shivered, her teeth chattered, her throat tightened, and she wheezed.

Breathe, Melissa. Relax.

She went back to her room, flopped onto the bed, and curled into a fetal position under her blanket. Her body jerked at every noise. Hours went by before she slept again.

Chapter 16

Monday night, Dwight and Jim spent some time hand-digging the rest of the dirt off one of the coffins so the backhoe wouldn't ruin it. It wasn't what Jim wanted to see, but wrote on the map it was full of old dishware wrapped in cloth for protection.

His temper rose. He'd gotten a message on the funeral home's phone from Carlos. He was the big-wig in New Mexico and the due date for more Twist was coming up. It was a threat spoken in a pleasant tone of voice. But it wouldn't last long.

Jim got the backhoe started and went out to the farthest mark in the field, close to Ginger Lane. He couldn't drive a straight line because of the marks of the other spots. He thought it would be a hard path to follow, even on a motorcycle.

An hour later, with the coffin lid up, Jim howled. Not a good thing to do, but had to get his anger out. The coffin was empty. All the hard work for nothing. He shut the lid and reburied it. *The saying about the third time being a charm had better come true on the next one,* he thought.

Dwight grew impatient, too, and did more shovel throwing instead of digging. It took longer to dig up the next coffin. It was in deeper, and he ran into rocks causing more dirt to fall and cover what he had dug up.

In the end, it was a waste of time; another empty coffin. Jim and Dwight were done for the night. To keep on the clear side, they decided to dig more on Friday night.

"All this digging has made me pretty thirsty. How about you?" Dwight had hope in his voice. He shut the passenger door to Jim's car and fastened his seatbelt.

"Depends. Why?" He put his car in gear, drove out of the field onto the main road, and headed downtown towards the funeral home.

"There's Fat Rat's, a bar by the train depot. Ugly, dirty place with cheap buzz and hot chicks." Dwight's voice perked up. He turned to look at Jim. "It's on the corner of 1st and 12th Avenue."

Jim agreed and parked on the street in front of Fat Rat's door as they arrived. He parked close to the front of the bar and hoped it was as good as Dwight said it was. They walked in the door and Jim stopped for a second. The place was packed with locals and country music blasted through the speakers.

Dwight led Jim to a booth back in the corner which blocked out some of the noise. A bowl of peanuts sat in the middle with an empty one on the side to put the shells in. A few seconds later the waitress approached them with a menu. "What can I get you tonight? You want the usual Dwight?"

"Hi, Peggy. The usual Draft and I feel like your special ham sandwich." He deshelled a couple peanuts and chewed them. "Anything for you, Jim? My treat."

"I'll take what he's having." Jim looked and Dwight. "You're a regular here?" He helped himself to the peanuts.

"More than I should be." He crunched another peanut. "Tell me how this business got started and how can you keep it going?"

Jim knew better to tell Dwight a revised version now before he got tipsy and said more that didn't have anything to do with the business. He tended to over talk when drunk, and if it sounded right to the listeners, most of it wasn't true.

Peggy brought them their orders. "Yell out if you need anything else." She winked at Jim and left.

Jim took a drink of his beer and cleared his throat. "My grandparents ran the business. They started with the funeral home, but it wasn't bringing in the money like they thought. My Grandpa was in Rotary and knew the city people. A couple of them got my family starting with counterfeit money back in the sixties thru the seventies.

"Got harder to make and they started working in drugs as the seller. Later, my grandparents, along with my parents, started experimenting with the drugs to make their own. Got a connection with people in New Mexico and our place in Nampa was the transfer station in between sites."

Dwight had finished his sandwich and half his fries were gone. "So, it took them years to create a good drug like Twist?"

"They had some second-rate drugs but it didn't pan out. When I died fifteen years ago, it was the best time for my family to move and let Nate take over. It was getting harder to cover their tracks and not get caught."

"Wow. All I can think of to say."

"Sounds good to me." They sat for another half hour and left.

Chapter 17

The rest of the week was a blur to Missy. She couldn't remember if she dreamed every night or if every day blended into one big nightmare.

On the bus to school on the last day, Ally scowled and folded her arms, "You'd think when Brandon picked up Kaleb, he'd take me, too."

"What do you mean?" Missy asked.

"See Brandon and Kaleb sitting on this bus?"

She glanced around. "No."

"Of course you don't. Brandon got a truck last night, and he's driving to school and took Kaleb." Ally raised her hands, like she was saying 'hallelujah'. "You'd think they could drop me off at South, but oh, no. Kaleb said forget it." She let her hands flop on her legs. "How rude."

Missy knew Ally would love to sit in the middle of the truck between her brother and Brandon.

Not a word from Maura in the seat behind them. Missy got close to the breaking point. An image flashed through her mind: she sitting next to Brandon. Nice. "Sorry, yeah, pretty rude. So, uh, what kind of truck?"

"Sweet, mid-sized, dark blue Chevy with a cherry on top. A five-year-old piece of pie." She blew a breath of resignation.

The school was set for a half-day with the last hour spent cleaning out their lockers, getting their yearbooks signed, and making promises to their friends to 'Stay in touch'.

Sitting at the lunch tables Julie said, "Here we're freshman, and had to go to a Jr. High with the seventh and eighth graders. We should've been in High School. This school system is weird."

"Doesn't matter now," Maura said as she signed Julie's yearbook "Nampa is behind. Next year the change will happen. South Jr. will become South Middle, 6th through 8th. Nampa High will get the freshmen."

On the bus ride home, Dr. J smiled and thanked Missy for the year of entertainment. She half smiled and got off the bus for good. Driver's Ed was planned during the summer, and driving a car to high school would be freedom.

After tossing her backpack on her bed, she took her yearbook with her into the kitchen. "Mom?" No answer. "Mom!"

Bang. A door swung shut in the basement. Missy went downstairs. "Mom, where are your and Dad's old yearbooks?"

"Yearbooks?"

"Yeah, yearbooks. You know high school yearbooks."

"Over in the corner on the bookshelf." Her mom pointed.

"'K." Missy headed over as her mom went upstairs. She looked at the top of the bookshelf and did a quick scan to the bottom. Bingo, she hit the jackpot and found two. She grabbed both and skipped back up to the kitchen bar.

Missy felt like comparing her yearbook to her parents to see what they wore in high school was different. Some of the hair and clothing styles were a hoot.

Her Dad's was first and it looked like he grew out of the popular feathered-hair look back in the late 1980s. It was in long layers all over his head like he blew it with a hairdryer. A lot of notes from girls like: 'Give me a call,', 'Let's have fun, XXOXOXO.' *Gross,* Missy thought and gave a disgusted look.

Mom's girlfriends left notes: "Glad we were friends," and "See you next year". There were notes from guys, too, but she didn't see anything impressive until one looked a little suspicious. It read, "My eyes will be watching you. You're forever mine. Jim.". Missy felt her skin ripple like Jell-O flooded her body. *Is this the Jim I heard my parents talking about?*

Mom came into the kitchen, "What are you doing?"

"Comparing your yearbook to mine and seeing what you looked like at my age. Back in the olden days."

"Olden days?" Mom laughed.

"Pretty old. At least no one is wearing *Little House on The Prairie* dresses." Missy touched her picture. "Hey, we look the same. Cool, eh?" Her mom peered over her daughter's shoulder.

"See?" Missy moved her yearbook page next to her mom's page. "We look like twins except for the eye color. Wickedly weird."

"Funny. I forgot I wore my hair long like yours."

"Mom, who's this Jim dude?"

"Jim dude? Why?"

"His note was spooky."

"What does it say?"

It seemed to Missy her mom's voice became a little tight.

"'My eyes will be watching you. You're forever mine. Jim'." She watched her mom take something out of the fridge.

"It was nothing. He was a year ahead of me and didn't live too far from here." She bit her lower lip. "He was a jokester, always flirting with the girls." Mrs. Mack looked at Missy with a forced grin and went quiet.

"What happened to him?"

She stopped for a minute; Missy watched her deciding whether or not to answer. Turning around, she said. "He died in a crash in the old field. It happened the summer after he and your dad graduated." She shrugged and left the room.

Wow. Missy looked at his photograph closer, and though it was small, Jim's eyes shined like car headlights. She got the same weird feeling she'd had on the night at the Tree Ditch. *Was his spirit roaming around the field? I remembered mom saying the name Jim the other night when I eves-dropped.*

Missy finished her comparison and put the yearbooks back on their spot on the shelf. She noticed her mom's sophomore book and grabbed it.

There were six photographs of her mom in this one with Jim. They were both wearing matching denim jackets, and on the front chest pocket was a horseshoe design. Underneath the photograph was the statement: "Jim and Vi, the perfect couple." And Missy's mom acted like she didn't know him!

"Hey, Mom." Missy went into her parents' walk-in-closet. Mrs. Mack was hanging up Dad's clean shirts.

"Yes?"

"Um, so, I want to ask you something."

"Ask." She kept hanging up Dad's shirts, smoothing them out on the hangers.

"How serious were you and Jim?"

Missy's Mom paused; her arm was stretched up to place the hanger on the rod. She turned to face Missy, looking a little pale. "Why?"

"Yearbook, sophomore year. I found you and him in there, too."

"Um, we were friends. As I told you, he liked to joke around a lot." She hung up another shirt.

Six pictures? You are forever mine. Missy wasn't buying it. "What happened?"

She opened a drawer where she kept her socks and pulled out a one-pound box of See's candy.

"Nice." *Mom's secret stash.*

She took off the lid, picked one up, and handed over the box to Missy who selected a chocolate-covered cashew. She shrugged. "We went out for a while, but we went our separate ways."

There was more to it. Missy could tell, and leaned against the door frame, finishing her candy, licking her fingers to show appreciation. "Still got the jacket?"

Missy's mom offered her another candy. Missy shook her head. "You sure?"

"Yep."

Her mom grabbed one more, put the lid back on the box, placed it back in the drawer, and bumped it shut with her hip. Missy could tell she was thinking.

"4-H," she said, more to herself, and sat on the side of her bed. Missy followed. "There were five groups of four, and each group had their own matching symbols stitched onto the jackets." She ran her hands over the bedspread. "Don't remember why, but my group wanted a horseshoe embroidered on the pocket."

"Still have it?"

Mrs. Mack looked at Missy, seemingly wondering how much she should tell her of her past. Sometimes secrets were better left buried.

She went over to her cedar chest, the one she kept covered with Missy's grandma's beautiful quilt. She lifted the lid and the quilt glided off, landing on the floor with a soft thump. Sifting through folded clothes as though she didn't know what she would find, Missy could see her mom's body tremble. Her hands stopped moving. "Guess I do." Lifting it out, she handed Missy the jacket.

Missy put it on; it fit perfectly.

Missy's mom brushed down the sleeves, straightening out the creases. "You can borrow it."

Missy smiled. She was now in possession of the coolest jacket ever.

Chapter 18

Later, Julie came over to spend the night at Missy's house. She would have had Maura and Ally come over too, but Maura went out of town and Missy didn't want a threesome.

They stood at the kitchen counter waiting for the popcorn.

"Don't forget," Julie said. "I like lots and lots of butter."

"Lookie, I melted tons." Missy scooped out a heaping cup of brown sugar from the bag, added it to the pot and stirred.

Julie raised her voice a notch, "I love caramel corn."

"I think it's done. Bring it over here. I'll do the honors."

Julie brought the bowl over. Missy drizzled the caramel on and stirred. The aroma of buttery sweetness filled the kitchen. "Smells like heaven." Julie sighed.

"Mmmm, mmmmm good."

Missy poured in the rest of the sauce and did a final mix. Grabbing a big spoon, she filled it with popcorn, dripping with caramel, and shoved it in Julie's mouth.

"Clip clop, clip clop." Tommy galloped into the kitchen. "I smell it, I smell it. I want some!" he raised the blue bowl from the table.

"Oh, no you don't." Missy snatched the bowl from him. "Yours is over there, the red one."

Tommy peered into the bowl and looked up with a frown. "There's no butter on it," he whimpered.

"Stop whining." Missy handed her bowl to Julie, opened the microwave and pulled out a dish of melted butter. Tommy grinned as he held his bowl for the topping. She poured the butter and stirred it. "There. Now leave."

Missy turned him around and shoved him off. He took a few steps and gave her a sneer before he went back to the family room.

"I'm impressed. No arguments," Julie said, as she watched Missy take clean glasses from the cupboard. "Since when?"

"I dunno. Sometimes we get along. He's not bad." She dropped ice into the glasses and got a big bottle of root beer from the fridge.

Settling into two overstuffed beanbag chairs, they placed the popcorn on the floor and had their own end tables for the soda. Perfect.

Julie would call Missy crazy because she loved scary movies. Aliens, action, zombies, and monsters made her laugh, as long as there weren't any ghosts. One of her favorite old movies from the 1980s was *The Thing*, and she knew Julie would love it, too.

"I'm not going to like this movie, am I?" Julie shivered. "The title sounds too creepy."

"Don't worry, there's nothing scary in it. Now quiet." She reached for the remote and hit "play."

After the movie and dealing with Tommy who tried to steal the caramel popcorn, Missy got up and grabbed her sleeping gear.

"Why in the world are we sleeping outside?" Julie wanted to know. "Creepy monsters will be waiting in the shrubs and hanging on the tree branches."

"I doubt it, and it wasn't scary." Missy rolled up her sleeping bag. "So, a head falls off, grows legs, and walks off upside down. We won't be attacked by one." She chuckled, thinking it was funny.

"Something could be under the trampoline."

"You're right." Winking at Julie she did the itsy-bitsy spiders crawl up her arm. "Small crawling bugs, spider webs, and dead leaves."

Julie tossed a pillow at her.

"Thanks a bunch. Let's head out."

"Does Tommy have a baseball bat?"

"Yes, but I don't know where it is right now."

"I like your trampoline being at ground level."

"I do, too. Easier to walk on. But if you drop something underneath it, it's a pain to get it. I've had to use a rake so many times to get something out."

They took turns spraying each other with bug spray, sleeping bags, and around the trampoline.

"The smell of this bug spray will keep a walking head away," Missy said.

"I doubt it. Why don't you look underneath and see if anything is there?"

"It would have to be a thin monster," she calculated the distance between the grass and the underside of the trampoline. "Let's see who can find the most falling stars."

After they got situated in their sleeping bags, they watched the sky. "Clear, no clouds, plenty of stars, the deals on," Missy said, as a full moon smiled down at them.

Missy couldn't get comfortable in her sleeping bag. As she started to fall asleep, sounds woke her up. A cricket chirped; a dog barked in the distance; she decided to think of Brandon.

Bright headlights glared in Missy's face. A tractor lumbered forward, closer and closer. She spun around on one foot and ran as fast as she could. This would be the best speed of breaking a track record getting the heck out of there. Something grabbed the back of her shirt and she swung her arm around to knock it away.

The tractor driver isn't going to get me, she grunted.

The driver grabbed her again.

"BrrBrbrbrTwok." The tractor was side by side with Missy. The driver reached his open hand out an inch from her face. She screamed.

"Missy, wake up," Julie said as she shook and pushed Missy around.

"Ugh," Missy grunted.

"Wake up."

"Huh? Oh." Missy opened one eye a slit. "It's you." She felt trapped inside a cocoon. The side of her face was lying on the thick plastic mesh of the trampoline. She tried to kick her legs but they were tangled up.

"You woke me up," Julie said.

"What?" Missy was still kicking like a bronco and forced herself to calm down. "Sorry."

"Sit still a minute."

Missy laid back and Julie helped her straighten out her sleeping bag.

"You hit me and made weird sounds."

"Sounds? Like what?"

"You were dreaming."

"You heard my dream?"

"Of course not. You were flapping your arms around and grunting. It was something like, 'r brbr thwok'," Julie sat up and wrapped her arms around her legs.

They were both contemplating Missy's noisy dream sounds when, "Brr brbrbrthwok".

They looked at each other; Missy knew they had both heard it.

"It's the same weird noise," Julie said.

Missy took a deep breath. "I think it's the tractor from my dream, I was running from it. Something held me so I kicked to get away."

"Well, now I'm hearing it too, for real. So, is this one of those *Twilight Zone* things where your dreams become reality? I don't like the sound of it."

"Brr brbrbr thwok".

The sound was coming from the far end of the field.

"This is no T.V. program. I don't care if it is *The Twilight Zone* to me. I am going to go see for myself." Missy sat up and put on her shoes.

A worried look crossed Julie's face. "See what?"

"The shack."

"Are you crazy?"

Maybe she was, but now she didn't care. "Come on, Nancy Drew." Missy stood and folded her arms. "I'm going and so are you."

"No flippin' way. It could be anything, and whatever it is, it isn't anything good. No siree. I plan to enjoy my sophomore year."

Missy could see she was doing this wrong, scooted over and put her hands together. "Pretty please with sugar on top?"

"No." Julie shook her head.

"You keep moving your head it will fall off and grow legs."

"Not funny. I'm scared."

"We'll be careful. I promise. A pinky promise." Missy reached over, hooked her pinky with Julie's and tightened the grip.

Julie puffed out, "O-o-h-k-k-kay."

Julie put on her sneakers and they tiptoed to the gate on the side of Missy's house. She unlatched the gate and the hinge uttered a screech, shattering the stillness.

"Great," Julie mumbled. "Let's wake up your parents."

"Please, let's not," Missy muttered, and looked at the darkened bedroom windows. *No lights. Good.* The gate swung open the rest of the way in blessed silence.

Lights shone ahead, and a low growling sound grew closer. Missy stopped short and Julie bumped into her, grabbing Missy's arm and yanking her into the shrubbery. "It's coming after us," she screeched. A car sped by and disappeared. Julie rested her head on Missy's shoulder.

Missy nodded. She shivered. "You're not going to chicken out on me, are you?"

"Aren't you scared?"

"Yes," she admitted. "But I'm tired of being scared. I've been scared for so long, I'm worn out. Now I'm curious to see what's going on. Someone is up to something."

They peered over the bushes and saw nothing. They slipped beyond the bushes and a minute or two later stood at the dirt pit's edge.

"I changed my mind about seeing the shack. That's where the backhoe is."

"I don't like this either way," Julie moaned.

"Shush. You'll be fine." They crept halfway down the dirt path.

"Click. Click. Click."

Missy gasped and Julie whimpered.

"Getting tired of strange sounds," Julie whispered. She gripped Missy's elbow.

"No kidding. Maybe it's a ghost playing the drums?" She made Julie let go of her.

"Funny." Julie braced her hands on Missy's shoulders. "I'm going back."

"We're doing this together."

What had been a clear sky now was covered with dark cotton ball clouds. It made the path harder to follow as they felt their way with each footstep. It was narrow and steep, but there was more. Something else made Missy feel the same way she felt at the Tree Ditch. Uneasy.

Missy grabbed Julie's arm. By the end of the night, they'll both have bruises from shoulder to wrist. "I have a weird feeling we're being watched."

"Stop freaking me out and let go. If we're going to do this, let's do it." Julie moved away and tripped on her own feet, but didn't fall.

They continued to an old mattress aging at least twenty years old with not much cushion left. They sat and waited in silence.

As Missy's eyes adjusted to the darkness, she noticed the familiar shapes of miscellaneous junk scattered around. There was a pile of Playboy magazines stacked up on the side of the mattress facing the tree. *So gross.*

She looked up to the bank of the pit where a rusted ruined tractor sat, it was upright on its wheels, but the top and sides were smashed and caved in on the front. Something flashed in the side window. Missy clutched Julie's leg.

"Ouch, let go."

It happened once more; this time light went through the front window. Missy pointed to the tractor. Julie didn't see it.

"What's wrong?"

The third time, Julie saw it and shot Missy a panicked look.

"Someone's up there," Missy whispered. "It could be the driver of the tractor."

They scooted together as close as they could as time stood still.

Click. It sounded like a light switch on the wall.

They couldn't tell where it came from, because the sound was deadened inside the pit.

"Now I'm past scared," Julie announced, as her eyes searched for where the noise had come from.

The light flashed again, crossing their faces.

Frantic, Missy felt around the mattress for means of self-defense. Half buried in leaves and debris laid a short, thick branch. She grabbed it and hefted it for weight.

Yup, this'll do.

She felt sort of ready to defend herself.

"The light's getting closer, look," Julie said in a tight whisper.

Missy held the branch at the ready. "You come any closer and I'll knock your head off."

The footsteps closed in and a figure stood before them, beyond the reach of the mighty stick. A flashlight shone on their faces.

"I told you, I'll knock your brain out. Leave us alone." Missy raised her voice.

"Don't hit. It's me," a male voice said, the flashlight blinding them.

"Me who? I don't know any me beside myself. Get the light off our faces and watch it. We've got a weapon." Julie whimpered and covered her eyes.

"Weapon?" He took a step closer.

111

"Stay back," Missy said. "We can defend ourselves." She swung the branch back and forth, hoping to prove how dangerous it could be.

"Hey, chill. I'm not a ghost or a monster." The figure turned the flashlight on himself.

Missy gawked. "Brandon?"

"Brandon?" Julie looked at Missy for a second. "Prove it."

"See? It's me."

It was. Oh, man, Missy felt like a dope.

"Why are you out here in the middle of the night?" Julie growled. "Are you following us?"

"I was jogging, heard a weird noise, and came to look around. We did Neighborhood Watch where I used to live," he explained.

Missy tried to say something, but nothing came out except a little squeak. Julie turned and looked with a surprised expression.

Brandon stepped up beside Missy on the mattress. "Sorry I scared you. You're looking at me weird."

"Nnooo," she said. "We're here for the same reason. We were sleeping on the trampoline in my backyard and heard weird noises, so we came to look." She remembered to drop her stick.

Julie focused on Brandon. "I know you. You're friends with Kaleb. I'm Julie."

"Hi," he said.

"I'm Missy." Her heart fluttered.

"I know. We've met."

Julie looked at her.

"Homework at Ally's."

Julie raised her hands, "I wasn't there," she stated in a sarcastic voice.

"Oh yeah." Missy scrunched her nose, making little wrinkles. "I'll fill you in later," she said to Julie, then looked at Brandon. "How can you hear noise from here when you live on the other end of the neighborhood?"

"I jog around the neighborhood kind of late when I can't sleep."

"So, you know what it is?" Missy hoped she wasn't the crazy one in the neighborhood, hearing things.

"I think someone's driving a backhoe and wonder why they do it late at night and wanted to see." He looked at the wrecked tractor. "The backhoe on the field was running at the back of the field and didn't want to be noticed, so I figured I'd see the one you talked about in your English paper," Brandon looked at Missy.

"Glad I'm not the only one hearing things."

"I don't care if it *is* a backhoe. It doesn't sound nice," Julie said.

Missy could feel Julie squirm on the mattress.

Brandon agreed. "No, it doesn't."

Missy looked around and noticed they hadn't heard the noise since Brandon showed up.

"Could be done for the night, whoever it is. Farming at night, though, is weird," Brandon said."

Missy stood, "I don't think its farming, but it isn't good."

A cool breeze whisked past the kids, sending dust and leaves in a tiny whirlwind. It scampered up the slope and spun around the big rear wheels of the dilapidated tractor. The debris continued beyond the machine, dancing around the outline of a figure whose long hair rose on the breeze. The figure stood there while the debris moved around it. The breeze settled and the debris, too. When it did, there was no one there.

Julie and Brandon looked at each other, then at Missy.

"I'm done. I've had enough for one night. Let's get the heck out of here," Missy said.

Julie sprang up. "I'm creeped out."

"Did you see it?"

"I did but I prefer to think we didn't see anything," Julie said.

"I saw something," Brandon admitted, "but I couldn't say what."

"I think we need to split. If my parents look outside and see we're not on the trampoline, there'll be heck to pay."

Brandon nodded.

A flash of light caught Missy's peripheral vision. *Now what?* She glanced up to the tractor and thought she saw something, but if there was anything there, it was black. So, whatever it was, it was gone now. A cold, empty feeling ran deep into her bones. *They say ghosts leave a trail of cold air. Were there ghosts here in the pit? Was Jim watching over them?*

"Missy, what are you waiting for?" Julie reached out to grab the front of her shirt and she pushed her hand away.

"You're in front, so start moving," Missy snapped.

Brandon stood inches behind Missy, close enough to feel his warm breath tickling her ear. "Ladies," he said. "Julie. You lead the way." He touched Missy's arm. She glanced up and caught his grin. He had a cute smile.

Julie turned, and they followed her.

"No tripping," Missy said. Although tripping was her thing, not Julie's.

Brandon whispered, "I'll catch you if you do."

Missy was glad it was dark. She didn't want him to see her smile.

The short walk back to the house was silent. Julie was on one side and Brandon on the other side of Missy. It seemed he purposely made contact with Missy's arm; she felt fireworks at each touch.

The three stood in the driveway. Brandon hesitated. His eyes lingered on Missy's. "It was nice meeting you two, even under these circumstances." He grinned. The boy had a sense of humor. He gave Julie a nod and looked back at Missy.

"Never. Hear me? I'm saying this in front of Brandon, so I have a witness. Never ask me to go there again," Julie snarled.

Missy felt terrible for Julie. She had promised her it was safe, the backhoe noise, the maybe ghost, but it wasn't an afternoon picnic. Maybe they didn't have any business there.

"I've had worse evenings," Brandon said without explanation. "See you around." He left. After five steps, he turned around and waved. He crossed the street and kept going.

The girls got back to the trampoline and settled in their sleeping bags.

"Positive it was human?" Julie asked.

"No. Well, maybe. I don't know. Head on top, hair, two legs and arms like a human." Missy stopped. "I wouldn't like to think we saw a real ghost. Whatever it was," she exhaled, "it was different."

"Too different for me. I meant what I said. I'm never going back there at night. No. Never, under any conditions. Remember? No wonder you complain about your creepy dreams."

"I guess." Missy fluffed her pillow and made herself more comfortable.

Julie sat up in her sleeping bag. "I can tell he likes you."

Missy shrugged. "No, he doesn't. He felt sorry for me."

"You wish. He likes you." She smiled. "Night, Missy." Julie laid and turned her back to Missy.

Missy curled up in a ball. She didn't want to think of Brandon, but had a hard time controlling her mind on how to feel about him. She wouldn't mind talking to him about his thoughts of seeing the figure by the tractor. Was it the driver who died in the crash? First, it wasn't there and then it was. Ghosts know how to come and go, right? Missy tried to remember if there was a lot of light from the moon or if there was a reflection coming off one of the tractor's broken windows. The breeze. Where did it come from? There was no breeze tonight. The air was still.

Too much caramel corn and going boy-crazy. One thing she didn't like. Too many bad dreams.

Chapter 19

Another cloudy night and Jim sat on the backhoe with Dwight standing by. Jim's time was running out for the items and drugs, and the pressure was driving him crazy. If he kept finding empty coffins, he'd consider running off to New Mexico or Spain.

He'd been dreaming about Violet most of the nights and what their future together would've been like if she hadn't dumped him for Ray.

Jim started as Dwight yelled out, "What are you trying to do squish me? Look where you're digging." Jim stopped the backhoe and surveyed the damage, then moved his digging line.

Jim readjusted the controls and lifted two more scoops of dirt. The next grip hit the coffin. It didn't sound as hollow as the others. "This is it. This is the treasure."

"I heard it loud and clear," Dwight said, and swung his arms above his head. He watched Jim scoop the last dirt off the coffin.

Jim got out with a crowbar. "Don't get your hopes up. With my luck, it's full of more dishes or antique books."

Jim cranked the latches loose and lifted the lid. He was right; more dishes, but also a decent amount of Twist. He had a couple of connections in Nampa to get some real cash. The sad part was, the instructions and equipment to make Twist weren't there. More digging to do, but Jim would be on the happier side now.

"How many more coffins are there?" Dwight asked.

"Done for tonight. I saw a bunch of kids walking to the pit."

After they removed the supply of Twist, Jim lowered the coffin back into the ground and recovered it. Next, he marked it on the map of what items were still in there. "Five maybe six. But there could be more. If we can't find the parts, there has to be another place. I'm trying to figure out where."

They walked to the shack where Jim sat on the cot and sniffed some Twist. His mood sharpened, focusing his thoughts.

"When are you going to come in contact with your buyers?" Dwight paced around the shack sniffing his supply of Twist.

"Tonight. Another reason we are done, and have a small supply. I thought of many excuses of why I didn't have any to trade but now I'm safe."

"Where?"

"Down by the train depot." Jim got up and prepared to leave.

"Good place. Nice and dark. Nobody hangs around there at night."

Jim shook his head. Dwight was a good guy, but clueless in most things. The North part of town was busy at night with distractions. He wouldn't stand out doing the trading.

They got in Jim's car and drove to town. To kill sometime, they stopped at Red Steer to get a drink. Jim hoped Ruth would be working, but she wasn't.

Across the street from the Train Depot were parking lots on both sides of the road. Jim parked kiddy-corner from the Depot in an open lot. He pointed out the driver's side window. "See the small door on the side of the wall? It's the door to the underground tunnel. We will meet my contact by it."

Dwight looked and never realized it was there. He'd lived in Nampa most of his life but never did anything extra to know what excited or not. "Underground tunnel? I never knew."

"Now you do." Jim got out of the car and grabbed his briefcase full of Twist.

"Is it like in the movies where they carry a briefcase with all the cash and you have to count it out first? Do you go to your car or hide behind a building?" Dwight acted like a nerdy kid and followed.

Jim tried to mellow out Dwight. "First off, it's not a big exchange. It's more like a hand off. Second, if you don't calm down, you'll draw attention."

"I'll stay cool and not say a word." Dwight did an imaginary zipping his lips shut.

Jim rolled his eyes as he led the way to the stair's door.

They didn't have a long wait. Within five minutes Jim saw his contact person fast walking toward him. He looked a little on the edge and darted his eyes all over the place.

"We're safe. Got the money?" Jim asked.

"I almost didn't come but had no way to get ahold of you." Sweat dripped down the man's face. "I'm feeling like the middle man. You know, the one that ends up killed."

"Why, Zack?"

"Rock's Edge is trying to take control of the gangs in Caldwell and Nampa along with the head drug distributors. They are causing problems." He rubbed both hands on his legs to dry off the sweat. "My cousin Daren is in Rock's Edge and he along with some of the gang members are pressuring me to join.

"I feel like I'm being watched twenty-four/seven. I left tonight and Daren happened to be driving by my house. He rolled down his window and asked where I was going this late at night. I told him the store. I feel like he's following me around. If he sees me with you, who's dead? We both will be." He pointed at Jim. "Really dead. Oh, and by the gang's luck, they know you're alive, too. I wonder if your cousin Nate spilled the beans when he told them off last year."

Jim massaged his forehead and Dwight stood there, not sure what to do or say.

"I left the money in the trunk of my car. I want to be safe. For all I know my cousin is standing by it when I go back."

Jim inhaled and let out his breath slowly to try and stay calm. "Can we do it tomorrow night, same time same place?"

Zack's head nodded fast like a bobble-head doll. "Ya, sounds good." He turned and half jogged down the road.

The trading had gone sour, and Jim needed a drink.

Chapter 20

"Wake up, wake up!" Tommy yelled as he ran out the back door of the house.

"Argh," Missy growled.

"What?" Julie rolled over, half awake.

"Tommy."

"Wake up!" Tommy leaped on the trampoline and jumped around. "Mommy made pancakes."

"Ugh." Julie disappeared deeper into her sleeping bag.

"Stop jumping." Missy sat up, groggy. "What time is it?"

"Don't know." Tommy jumped off and ran back into the house.

The girls dragged themselves into the house, smelling pancakes and eggs.

"Good morning, girls," Mrs. Mack said.

"Morning," Julie mumbled.

Missy nodded. Her head felt like a block of wood.

Missy's mom looked at her. "Did you stay up all night talking?"

"No." It wasn't a lie; she had tossed and turned a lot.

She grinned and handed over plates stacked with pancakes. "The syrup's on the table."

"Nice," Julie said, coming to life a little. "Thank you."

The table was loaded with all the essentials. Missy's mom knew she liked sliced bananas and whipped cream on hers. There was a bowl of each. Julie's preference was a Plain Jane. A couple pats of butter and a squiggle of maple syrup dripped across the top.

Julie devoured her pancakes, and Missy took a couple of bites. It didn't taste sour like her life was going. She wasn't sure if she should tell her mom or Julie about her dreams. Well, Julie knew about some, but not details about all of them.

Mrs. Mack put a bottle of orange juice on the table. "So, ladies, what are your plans for today?"

Julie swallowed, "My family is going to go look at a new horse. I'm thinking of joining 4-H this coming school year. They have summer meetings, so I'll give it a try."

"Sounds exciting. Where is the horse?" Mrs. Mack asked.

"Horseshoe Bend. Kind of a funny place to go get a horse."

"Leave it to Idaho with the strange names," Missy said.

Tommy was eating at the counter. "Mom, why is it that name?"

"If you look at a map, the river outlining the town is shaped like a horseshoe."

"Oh."

Julie took a drink of the orange juice to help wash her breakfast down. "I need to get going. It's about an hour drive pulling the trailer and my parents wanted to leave early." She grabbed her bedding. "Thanks for the breakfast and I'll talk to you later, Miss."

They high-fived and Julie left.

Tommy came over and looked at Missy's plate. "Can I have your pancakes?"

Their mom saw Missy's plate was still full. "Do you have an upset stomach?" She touched Missy's forehead and noticed the dark circles under her eyes.

Missy shook her head lightly. "No. Not hungry." To show thanks she drank most of her orange juice. She went to her bedroom and put on shorts, a T-shirt, socks, and shoes. She needed a break to clear her mind.

Missy got on her motorcycle and drove through the neighborhood. She slowed down as she approached Brandon's house. *I wonder what he thinks about last night at The Pit?* Her curiosity had gotten the better of her. On the other hand, Missy didn't want him to think she was interested. Way too dangerous. His truck was parked under the carport. *I wonder what he's doing?* She knew there was no finding out, so she did two extra laps on the inner roads of the neighborhood and went home. Tommy greeted her in his Native American outfit with cowboy boots on.

"Will you take me for a ride, Missy?"

"Sure. But you have to keep a sharp eye out for any bad cowboys chasing us."

125

"You bet." He hopped on the back of the bike and wrapped his arms around her tight. Missy was glad he wasn't strong yet, or he would have squeezed the air out of her.

"Can we stop at the tree by the ditch so I can dig?"

"Dig? For what?"

"Arrowheads."

"I doubt there are arrowheads in the field." She moved a little to make him loosen his grip. It didn't work. He still squeezed tight.

"Uh, loosen your grip, chief. There you go. The driver needs to breathe."

"Yuh, there are," he said, tapping her back to see if she could hear. "The Indian Chief said it was an old graveyard."

"You talked to a Native American Chief?"

"Yep. On our field trip last week," he said.

Must have been an excellent field trip, Missy thought, *getting one of the local Native Americans to dress up.* "Do you know why they call the fields by the Tree Ditch and The Pit 'A Misty Field'?"

"Nope."

"Because it's got ghosts."

"I don't care. I'm not scared."

Missy snorted. "You should be. They say spirits are roaming around out there. People say they've seen them in the morning before the sun is up. The ghosts walk around while the mist covers the field."

"Think we can see them now?" Tommy sounded excited.

126

"I doubt it. Now you can hold on tight. I'm giving you a good fast ride."

Tommy laughed and squealed with excitement as Missy drove on the path to the tree ditch and put down the kickstand by the tree. "Start digging. We can't stay long." Missy sat by the tree.

Tommy searched for a small pile of dirt by the field. "Will it make the ghosts mad if I dig?"

"Why would they be mad?"

"Maybe they don't want to share."

Tommy thinks he knows how to share, ha. "I think we'll be fine."

While under the tree, Missy drifted into sleep. She dreamed of last night when she met Brandon at the bottom of The Pit. *He must be a nice guy to everyone he meets. When he touched people,* she wondered, *how many times has he felt Ally's back or arm when he was over at Kaleb's?*

Missy woke with a start and looked where Tommy had been digging. He wasn't there. He'd walked into the middle of the field, looking at something Missy couldn't see. "What are you looking at? A fox or gopher?"

He didn't answer and stood still. *Unusual for Tommy,* she thought.

"Tommy." Still nothing. She walked to where he stood, put her hand on his head and rustled his hair. "Hey there, Space Cadet, what's going on?"

"I think the Native Warrior is sad."

"What?"

He continued to stare into the middle of the field. She took his hand and tugged him back to the dirt bike.

"He seemed sad because someone is digging in his field."

"How do you know?" Missy kick-started the cycle.

"He was standing over there," he pointed to a spot in the field. "But I think he didn't mind me digging. I think he likes me." He opened his hand and showed Missy an arrowhead. "See. He showed me where to find it."

"You got it here?"

"Yep." Tommy hopped on behind Missy.

"When?"

"While you were at the tree."

She hadn't seen anyone but Tommy digging with the small trowel he brought with him.

Tommy was quiet on the ride back, not his usual self. Missy dropped him off at the front door and parked the dirt bike in the garage. Lowering the kickstand, she rested her arms against the handlebars. Her little brother had a good imagination. On the other hand, she'd heard ghosts would trust little kids more than grownups. Did he see a ghost?

How could she think he hadn't? *Look what happened to me, Julie, and Brandon last night at the pit.*

What went on in quiet, dull, old Nampa? Backhoe sounds, flashing lights, not coming from Brandon's flashlight, and ghosts. At least one.

***

Later at night when Missy and Tommy were in bed, their parents had a conversation in the bedroom.

Mrs. Mack pulled her pajamas out of the drawer. "Ray?"

"Yes." He sat on his side of the bed. "What is it? I can tell you're bothered."

She joined him on his side. "I'm worried about Missy. She's not eating much and has lost some color. She says she's not sick but I'm concerned."

"A growing phase?"

"No. Right before I had my run in with the Jim look-alike, I've seen and heard her in her sleep moving and grunting." She patted her husband's leg. "It's almost like she can sense trouble."

"I can't blame you for watching too many television shows at night on mysteries." He said. "David, my friend from KTNP came in yesterday and gave me general information about the gang Rock's Edge. They've been acting up with violence and damage to run-down houses in Caldwell, and moving closer to the Nampa border."

"I've seen State Troopers, Police Officers, and unmarked cars from who knows where driving by our house and down Ginger Lane, day and night." Mrs. Mack scratched her head.

Mr. Mack nodded. "I've seen them during the early morning when the fog is light as I get ready for work. They don't drive by twice a month, but this is weekly."

"I wonder if it has to do with the gang. Or if there are any in Nampa we don't know about, with kids in Missy's grade. Maybe she had a run into some bullying at school and won't tell us."

"It doesn't hurt to ask."

Mrs. Mack thought for a minute before continuing. "What if Jim never died? What if I did see him at Paul's?"

"Still bugging you?" Mr. Mack looked content, but if his wife looked at his face, she could tell he was hurt.

She nodded and went to her side of the bed. "I feel like doing some snooping around myself to make sure my mind isn't playing tricks on me."

"You know better, Vi. Good night."

Jim used to call me Vi, too.

They snuggled together in bed and fell asleep. At least Mr. Mack did.

Chapter 21

Sunday through Friday morning, it rained. Missy got together with Julie once, but the rest of the time she stayed in her room reading when there weren't any good T.V. shows scheduled. She did play a couple of Game Cube games to keep Tommy entertain as well.

Missy did notice during the week of the rain, she only had one bad dream. Her mom asked her each day during the week if she was feeling okay or needed to talk. Missy couldn't tell her mom; she wouldn't understand.

Friday afternoon, Missy got a call from Maura. "Our two-week vacation turned into a six-day flood."

"Serious?"

"Yes. We got the same rainstorm Nampa got. So, we were in a cabin, but it was a small cabin. No space and everyone got tired of playing board and card games."

Missy agreed. She'd get bored or go utterly crazy crammed in a room if she had a sister along with a little brother. "Must have been a hundred-mile-wide rain cloud covering the area."

"Pretty sure it was. So, the American Parade is tomorrow and my mom insists we go, so do you want to come, or is your family going?"

Missy knew she was a fill-in for Ally since she was still out of town. "Sure. We haven't been for a while. What time?"

"Pick you up around 9:00 am. It starts at 10:00 but we want to find a good parking place."

"I'll be ready on time." Missy hung up the phone. *I would have gone with Julie but she's in the parade on her horse. I'll cheer her on when she passes me.*

***

Jim and Dwight took a trip to the field Friday night to see if the ground had dried up enough to dig. The clouds had cleared and he was tired of sitting around. If he dug another hole in a marked place on the side closest to the lake, he probably wouldn't be noticed.

Jim's contact Zack had freaked out again last Saturday and didn't get a sale until Monday night in the pouring rain. Zack still was on edge, worried about being watched. He set up another time to meet in a couple days.

Jim's parents called several times during the week putting on the pressure. "You need to work faster Jim; our contractors are putting the weight on us. Soon they will be tracking you down." His mom's voice pleaded in his ear. "Carlos is losing patience."

His dad was blunt, "Day, night, rain, snow, sleet, slush, you dig up those coffins. If people ask, you tell them you're searching for your grandparents' antiques and treasures. You will be hunted and forced to do it by our Mexican contacts, let alone the gang in Caldwell soon, if you don't produce."

"Thanks, Dad, I love you too." Jim ended the conversation with bitter sarcasm.

Jim couldn't look at his parents as a loving type. More as a game player, and Jim was their lucky piece.

"I guess those were your parents?"

"Bingo. Feel the pressure? I do."

Dwight nodded.

Chapter 22

Maura rang Missy's doorbell Saturday morning, "Come on, we're running late." She hurried back to her mom's car. Missy followed.

"Where's Sandy and Jack?" Missy asked.

"Being a pain. They thought they had better things to do than waste their time at the Parade of America."

Mrs. Derringer tried to cover bad thoughts. "They are working on cleaning out the garage."

Maura looked at Missy and rolled her eyes.

They found a spot three blocks from the main road. Maura's mom went her way, and Missy and Maura went the other, towards Missy's dad's office.

They were moving with the flow of people when Maura elbowed Missy. "Missy, look, there's Brandon and Kaleb."

"Where?"

"If you look to your left now, you'll see them."

The crowd gathered, but Missy craned her neck and spotted them. She made eye contact with Brandon and nearly tripped.

"Ugh," Missy groaned as she stumbled. A strong arm went across her in time to save her from falling face first on the cement. She didn't want to go under those feet. "Uh, uh, thank you."

Missy looked up into a pair of the bluest eyes, the same uncommon color as hers. The eyes looked back in a mesmerizing stare. She noticed a design on his denim jacket. A horseshoe!

In the next second, Maura grabbed Missy's arm and jerked her upright. "My heck, Missy, you are such a klutz. Tripping on the bus, falling over hurdles. You're a danger to yourself and others."

Maura's words distracted Missy from checking out the man with the blue eyes and jacket. When she looked back, he was gone. "Did you see where he went?"

"Who went?" Maura wasn't interested. Missy shrugged, wondering if she had seen her own eyes looking back into hers.

They continued their search for a good place to watch the parade as Missy skimmed for the guy in the denim jacket, but he had melted into the crowd. While they waited, Missy let her mind wander. *The jacket designs. He had to be one of her mom's old 4-H buddies, unless he got the jacket at a rummage sale. And wow, his eyes were bright blue. He reminded me of the high school picture of Jim.*

"Are you going to the rodeo this year?" Maura interrupted Missy's thoughts.

"I doubt it. They seem lamer each year. The excitement has gone away."

"I agree." Maura turned her eyes up the street. "I heard the trumpet. The parade is on its way."

Sometime around the halfway point during the parade, while chewing on salt water taffy, Missy felt someone watching her. She thought it might be Brandon, and looked around trying to spot him, but no go. And there wasn't anyone else she knew trying to get her attention, so she dropped it. She was there to watch the parade.

Towards the last of the parade, Missy saw Julie with the 4-H club she had joined. Missy stepped into the street so Julie could see her. "Julie, Julie." She waved her arms.

Julie noticed and tossed out two big handfuls of candy directed to Missy. A few hit her legs and she tried to pick up a good supply, fighting against the other kids diving for it.

When the parade ended, Missy and Maura moved with the crowd back to where Mrs. Derringer parked. Missy wished Brandon and Kaleb had left their spot when she walked by. Feeling like a dweeb for tripping, she didn't need a reminder from Kaleb. Her wish didn't come true.

"Hey, Missy." It was Brandon.

She nodded to him and looked at Kaleb, who smirked.

"Don't trip over yourself," Kaleb said. "But if you do, I'll save you." He chuckled.

Today was not one of Kaleb's better days, and now Missy knew they both either saw her or were told. Major crap.

Brandon nudged Kaleb's arm with his elbow and gave Missy a sign with his hand and cell phone suggesting he'd give her a call later. Missy nodded, but didn't know if

Brandon thought Kaleb was funny or not. She crinkled her nose. Maura saw the gestures Brandon gave Missy and turned away. She kept quiet until they made it to the car. Within a minute, Maura's mom arrived.

"How'd you like the parade, girls?"

"With a horse-horse here and a cow-cow there." Maura was doing her "Old MacDonald" bit.

It was kind of funny, and Missy chuckled a little, but sometimes it didn't pay to be too enthusiastic around Maura, so she went into neutral. "Ducky."

"A total embarrassment," Maura said.

"What happened?" her mom asked.

Missy knew what was coming and opened her mouth to speak, but Maura butted in with her report. "Missy tripped in front of Brandon and Kaleb." She laughed.

It drove her crazy how Maura got pleasure out of another person's misery. If Maura's family moved, Missy would be in heaven.

***

Jim noticed the roads were blocked and walked to the store instead. But now something new was itching in his brain. When he caught the girl who almost tripped into him, he felt like he was looking at Violet when she was a teenager. There was something about the girl's eyes that stuck with him.

He made it back to the funeral home and stocked his mini-fridge with basics and a couple of beers.

The stress was putting more weight on Jim. They had dug up four deep holes in the field, and a shallow one yielding some drugs. Soon he wouldn't have time to squeeze in a dig. Jim seemed to get it done and gone before a police car drove by, but it still took too long. He needed to be able to dig for longer periods.

Waiting for the night wasn't working. Jim wasted valuable hours sitting around. In the meantime, he did a thorough search of the funeral home three more times, inside and out. He tapped the walls, yanked tiles out of the ceiling, and felt under the linoleum. He went outside and even dug a few holes with a shovel in the backyard, and still came up empty. He had turned himself into a mole for nothing in return.

Those parts have got to be here, Jim thought. *But where?*

Jim put his shovel away in the garage when he heard a knock on the front door.

"Hello. Hello?"

Click.

The door opened and shut. Someone had let themselves in. Brushing his dirty hands on his pant legs, he walked to the front office. It was Ruth.

"What brings you here?" Jim tried to be casual.

Ruth wore a strapless, pink-flowered sundress with her hair in a ponytail. A picnic basket in her hands. She was a pleasing sight.

"I saw your car parked out front." She held out the basket. "Thought you might be hungry."

Jim stood there with a blank face.

Her smile fell a bit. "I'll leave if you want, but here. Enjoy the food. It's a late Welcome Basket." She placed it on the desk.

Jim lifted the lid to take a peek.

She reached over and gave his hand a light, playful slap. "Hands off," she joked.

The aroma of fresh fried chicken wafted. "Smells good. Looks good, too." He lowered the lid and looked at her again. *Why not?* He thought. "Let's picnic here."

"Here?" She scanned around the office. "What are you doing?" she raised her eyebrows. The place was a mess. She saw ceiling tiles sitting in a small stack on the floor. In one corner by a filing cabinet, the linoleum had been peeled back. "Either you take your spring cleaning serious or you're looking for a treasure?"

He didn't answer. Way too close for comfort. Ruth wasn't stupid. Instead, he said, "Follow me," and winked. He took the basket by the handle in one hand and with the other, escorted her by the elbow to the garage. Releasing her arm, he stepped aside to let Ruth get the full effect of the coffin sitting in the middle of the room.

"A coffin?"

"Yup." He gave a slight nod. "Ever see one up close?"

"When I was eleven, my mom died. They had a viewing. It frightened me. I didn't like the idea of being caged in a box and buried in the ground." She shivered a little and placed her hand on the lid. "But now I think it's a little romantic." Ruth drew a little imaginary heart with her finger on the surface.

"Now it's a table." He took a clean towel from the shelf and spread it on top of the coffin. "Tablecloth."

"Charming. Chairs?"

He pointed to two metal folding chairs.

She stepped up closer and rapped her knuckles on one. "Comfy."

Jim placed the chairs one on each side of the coffin.

"Wait right here." He turned and went back to the front room. The small couch in the office had two thick cushions. "Perfect." With one in each hand, he carried them back.

"Here you go." With a satisfied smile, he placed one cushion on her chair and the other on his.

Ruth set the table. First, she got two cans of ginger ale. "Closest I could come to wine."

"I got beer," he offered.

"No!" she shouted.

Her response startled him. He sat up.

"Uh, sorry. It's a touchy subject. I'm not good with beer or hard liquor."

Jim nodded.

She rested her elbows on the coffin lid.

Jim didn't know what to say next, so he picked up the plastic silverware. "Looks good. Let's eat."

Ruth smiled and laid out the containers of food. She had packed fried chicken, mashed potatoes, buttered and salted corn on the cob, and coleslaw. They ate in silence.

Jim felt a little uncomfortable. He was usually fine around women since he took the upper hand. They liked him. He liked them a little less.

It's good to be ahead. Ruth's little outburst had put him off. He studied her as she took a bite of chicken. He did like her, a little. She wasn't a goody-two-shoes. She had a little grit, and she was easy on the eyes.

He knew she felt his gaze but kept her eyes on her plate. "My dad's an alcoholic. He yelled too much and life wasn't good around our house when I was growing up. Things are better now. I'm on my own." She took a drink of soda. "He's still alive. He sells cars and does alright at it, but when I was younger there would be times when the market wasn't good and he'd get depressed. Money problems, for one thing." She got up and paced around the room, came back and stood by the coffin-table.

"Does he still live in Nampa?" He wondered if Dwight was Ruth's father.

She nodded. "He's a loner, he and his old used cars he tries to sell."

It must be Dwight. Jim stood and placed his hand on her arm. "I'm sorry."

Ruth gestured with her free hand. "I'm fine. We still talk. Sometimes we have lunch or dinner together. I keep my distance. It's good enough the way it is."

She went back to eating with not much conversation. The food tasted good, but Jim didn't know what he wanted to do next, so he folded the towel and put it aside.

"Want to give it a test drive?" he pointed at the coffin and grinned.

"In there?"

"Yes," he smiled. "It's a coffin, with no dead body inside."

"Sure."

He helped Ruth put the empty paper plates in a bag and opened the lid. "Hop on in." and was glad he had put the fabric back in it.

Ruth looked like she might change her mind and fidgeted with the fabric. "Black velvet, huh." It wasn't a question. She lifted her leg and placed her foot on the bottom.

"Nice and sturdy. Built to last." He chuckled.

She glanced at Jim, took a breath, climbed in and laid on her back. She crossed her arm over her bosom. "This feels a little strange."

"Want me to close the top and bottom lids?" *Let's see if she'll trust me.*

"Go for it."

Jim closed the bottom lid with care and latched it. He stepped up even with her face and looked at her. "Having fun in there?" He rested his hands on the edge of the lid.

"You can pretend I'm Mysterio, the Magician. Now I'm going to close the other lid." He lowered it and latched the hook. "I know you can hear me in there. Enough air for you? Knock twice if you're good."

She knocked twice.

"If I was a magician, when I open the coffin, it would be empty and you'd come slinking down the middle aisle. The audience would be oohing and aahing."

She interrupted him. "Man, it's dark in here. Must be the velvet. There's not a hint of light."

He wondered how long he should let her stay in there. He got his answer in a few seconds.

"I'm ready to come out now. I've had enough."

"Certain?"

"Certain."

He unlatched the top lid, then the bottom. Ruth sat up and stepped out. "It's not Disneyland."

Jim nodded, but was kind of fun. Maybe he could have been a magician. Have a magic act and play Las Vegas. Hat and cape, swanking around the stage. Ruth could be his beautiful assistant, disappearing and reappearing. He stopped. What a total waste. What was he thinking of? He was a crummy con artist. End of story. End of illusions.

"Oh, I remember something," she said as she lifted the cushion. She nodded at Jim to copy and to follow her to the front part of the building.

"What?"

"Nampa has an interesting history. Back in the early 1900s, there was a lot of Chinese living here."

"Here in Nampa?"

"Yep. They came here because they were cheap labor and did a lot of work on the railroads. They knew if they could stay alive, they could make enough money to bring their family here from China.

"China was still a feudal society back then. America meant freedom way beyond anything they could expect back home. The poor wages were better than anything they could earn elsewhere. Most of the older buildings are in the same area as my antique store, you know? A few families did well enough to start a little business. They always worked hard. So, they brought their families here."

"You know your history." Jim did know about the underground tunnels, but the rest he didn't.

Ruth shrugged. "A little. Nothing others who live in Nampa don't know. But you didn't." She glanced at him.

143

"I didn't live in Nampa. Only one side of the family. My cousin's side. I grew up in Arizona. Came to visit a few times, but not enough to get to know the place or…." He didn't finish his sentence. *Boy, I'm getting good at lying.*

Ruth placed the cushion on the couch and sat on it; patted the space for Jim to sit next to her. He was taller so he put his pillow against the back and leaned on it.

"Did you know there are tunnels under those buildings?" asked Ruth.

"Are you serious?"

"There's an entrance to one in the basement at my store. It's not locked, but boxes are leaning against it now. The door itself is a little battered from age."

Jim's expression perked up. "Have you explored it?"

"I stepped in a few feet while I had light from the storage room. It felt eerie and didn't want to see any skeletons."

"You believe?"

"Not ghosts, of course, but skeletons? This is an old town."

"Hmmm. Are you scared of ghosts?"

"Nah. I'm scared of the living. Not the dead." She looked at her watch. "I've got to get going." She stood up. "This was fun."

Jim stood, too. "Thanks for the history lesson." He walked her to the door. "If you ever want to be buried for a second time."

"Once was enough." She gave him a quick smile.

Jim realized there was an undercurrent of hunger in her eyes. The truth was, he didn't know how interested he was in Ruth. His business here was more important, but she was a good-looking woman even if she was Dwight's daughter. He had been around the block a few times, but still, was happy enough with on-and-off relationships. The women he dated felt the same way, which made it easy. But there was something different with Ruth, and for a moment, he had the passing thought he didn't want to hurt her. Still, she wouldn't miss him when he was gone. She knew the score.

Jim set his hand under her chin and lifted her head. Leaning in, he gave her a small kiss on the lips, brushing his own against hers with the right amount of pressure. "Come any time."

"Maybe I will." She nodded and left without another word. He watched her walk away, her hips swaying hypnotically.

He closed the door behind her. A nice little interlude, but now he had work to do. First, see where those tunnels were located.

Chapter 23

The afternoon Missy got home from the parade, Julie and Maura came over and sat on the trampoline.

"You looked so in charge on your horse, Julie. Was it fun?" Missy asked.

"It was tolerable." She gave a devilish grin.

"Ah-ha, I think I know your look. Who is it?"

Maura, twisting her hair and playing it cool, "Do I know him?"

Missy could tell Maura was thinking if it was a good match or maybe some guy she should get to know first.

"Gabe Starke. He's in 4-H and lives down the street a couple of miles. His family breeds and shows horses. You should know who he is, Maura." Julie looked at her.

Maura raised her eyebrows. "I know he's a year ahead of us and moved to Nampa a couple years ago."

"Did you talk to him?" Missy poked Julie's arm.

"No. He might have a girlfriend." Julie frowned and looked at Missy. "When are you guys going to open the pool?"

"Within the next week, but first we need to do the yearly scrubbing of the pool cover."

"Sounds fun. Not."

"I know, but the benefits of seeing Kaleb and Brandon at Ally's pool will be worth it." Maura grinned and twisted her hair again.

"Are you ever going to cut your hair, Julie?" Missy got up and jumped.

Standing still in between jumps, Julie pulled her hair out of the ponytail and shook her head. "Nope, I like it long." Her black hair reached her waist.

"Does it tangle easy?" Missy asked.

"If it does, it doesn't matter. I'll know how to handle it." Julie braided her hair and tossed it back. Dramatic. Missy had to give her brownie points.

A few jumps and Maura broke the silence. "Remember last summer when you and I rode our horses by the lake?" She looked at Julie. "It took you hours to brush out the mess. Why didn't you braid it?"

"It would take the fun out of it. What beats the wind blowing through your hair?" Julie laughed. Missy noticed Julie had gotten braver as the summer went on and not letting Maura or Ally walk all over her.

"Ally is a pro at hairstyles from being obsessed with *Pinterest*. Maybe you should have her experiment with your hair since Ally's hair is too short for her to do anything with."

Missy and Julie glanced at each other in shock. This wasn't a common thing for Maura to say. What was she trying to do?

"Speaking of Ally, why didn't she come to the parade with us?" Missy asked.

"Had plans with her mom. I think they wanted to drive up to Sun Valley and go shopping." Maura looked back at Julie and waited for an answer.

"Nah, I like experimenting with my hair by myself." Sometimes Julie knew what to say to Maura. Missy was happy to let her handle Maura for a change. In the meantime, Maura kept bringing up Missy tripping in front of Brandon and Kaleb.

Missy was glad when Maura left. Unfortunately, Julie had to go home too.

Later in the evening she called Julie to see if she wanted to go motorcycle riding. She didn't. Since their little visit to the pit, she's noticed Julie had been distancing herself. Missy didn't think she had done anything to hurt Julie's feelings, but the way to know was to ask, but not tonight. Missy wasn't up for it.

When she thought about the four of them, it seemed to her Julie was her factual friend. Missy was positive she was more of a fill-in for either Ally or Maura when either of those two Bobbsey Twins weren't available. Missy decided she was done thinking for now, so she hopped on her dirt bike and cruised around the neighborhood.

She drove by Brandon's house. He and Kaleb were playing Frisbee in the front yard. Missy knew Brandon saw her because he let go of the Frisbee and sent it sailing off in the opposite direction. Kaleb had to go running for it. Brandon waved. *Did he want to see me?* Missy was game.

She drove into the driveway as Kaleb sprinted back with the Frisbee.

"Practicing Evel Knievel stunts?" Kaleb smirked. It seemed his brief interlude of good manners was over for the time being. Not even Brandon could cool Kaleb's reckless jets.

Brandon glared at him and looked back at Missy. "Want to throw the Frisbee with us? We could use another hand."

Hah. So, Brandon was her sponsor, huh? Missy grinned. It was her turn to have a little fun and decided to put on an act and pretend she wasn't good. "I guess. Haven't thrown one much, but if you can stand my bad tosses."

"We can handle it," Brandon assured her.

Missy parked the dirt bike and joined them on the front yard. Brandon and Kaleb spread out, Brandon went left, Kaleb to the right. She made up the third side to create a triangle.

Brandon threw it to Kaleb and Kaleb threw it back with a spiraling flip. *Oh brother. Kaleb thinks he's mister cool.* Missy faked a surprised look.

"See?" Brandon explained. "It's not hard. Keep your wrist straight and let go when the Frisbee's in front of you, it'll be a straight shot." He threw it to her and she caught it. Perfect.

Missy held it in front of her with a baffled look. Brandon decided to help and stood behind her. "Here, let me show you." He reached his arm around Missy and put his hand on hers. She twitched as tingles went through

149

her back. Good old light socket tingle. He didn't seem to notice.

"Now, bend your wrist back like this." He got closer to her back. "Flex it forward and now, let go," He let go, but Missy's hand stayed on until the Frisbee was in front of her. She let it go. It did a side glide and landed by her motorcycle.

"Oops." Missy smiled.

"You don't know how to do this, do you?" Kaleb laughed. "Oh, and try not to trip when you pick it up."

She was going to figure out how to make him choke on his remark before the afternoon was over. In the meantime, Brandon got back to his spot, and Missy retrieved the Frisbee.

"Your turn," Kaleb called. "You're too far away to get it to one of us. You need to scoot closer."

Ha. She looked at Kaleb. Little did he know. She played Frisbee with her dad. "I think I can." He had shown Missy some trick maneuvers, so she decided to do the Hook Thumber with a twist. She placed her thumb in the front inside the rim of the Frisbee and put her first two fingers rested on the rim. Missy tucked it under her chin and extended her arm towards Brandon. Using her thumb to provide the extra snap, she turned and aimed at Kaleb. The Frisbee went soaring and hit him in his gut. Nice and hard. He curled over.

"Sorry. Bad aim." Missy shrugged. But the jig was up. Brandon had caught on and they both laughed hard.

With a red face, Kaleb straightened up and said nothing. He knew it was no mistake. He had gotten the hint. Missy could hold her own.

They played for an hour. Missy showed them several of her moves, and how she was as good at throwing with her left hand as with her right. They were impressed and decided to call her 'Lefty' if they played again. Missy noticed Kaleb still had energy as if to run a marathon. *I wonder if he got hooked on Twist. I hope Brandon doesn't.*

Chapter 24

"Missy, it's time to get up. You've slept most of the morning." Her mom sat on the edge of Missy's bed and lightly shook her back. "Julie called a few times and said it was important."

"Umph." A noise but no movement.

"You've been a little pale the last week."

"Hangover from school withdrawal." Missy moved an inch.

Mrs. Mack got the phone and maneuvered it in Missy's hand. "And if you didn't have your phone on no-ring, it might have woken you up earlier." She exited but left the door open.

Missy pushed in the buttons on the phone with her eyes closed and hope it was the right number.

Julie answered. "Did you die and come back to life? You never sleep in."

"I wish. Didn't get to sleep until six o'clock." Missy rolled over and threw off the blanket.

"Reading your love story books?"

Missy wished it was the case. Sleep has become an enemy. She ignored the question. "What's so important?"

"My parents had a two-day business emergency in Nevada and left this morning. I didn't want to go with them. Can I sleep over again? I don't want to be by myself. And no sleeping on the trampoline."

"Scaredy cat." Missy laughed.

***

"Hey, everyone's asleep and we aren't." Missy smiled at Julie who sat on the other bean bag.

"So." Julie's eyes remained on the T.V., watching an old Shirley Temple movie.

"Want to do something fun?"

"I don't know." Julie eyed her with suspicion.

"Yes, you do." She got up, grabbed Julie's hand and hoisted her up.

"I don't think I'm going to like this," Julie said, but she followed Missy out the back door. Missy grabbed a pile of towels off the porch and carried them out the pool.

"Na-uh. No way, Jose."

"Nobody's going to see us. You stay at your end and I'll stay on this end." Missy tossed her a towel. "Easy to do. Put the towel on top of you as you take off your pajamas and underwear. See? Nothing's showing."

"That's so not like you. Besides, it's cold."

"Nope. The rain washed off the cover and my parents turned on the heat." She smiled. "Plus, it's a side you don't know about me yet. Ha ha."

"You're scaring me. Plus, what if someone sees us?"

"At one o'clock in the morning?"

Julie made it to the other side of the pool and repeated Missy's example.

"On the count of three, we close our eyes, drop the towel and jump in." Missy scooted closer to the edge.

In unison, they counted: "One, two, three." The towels dropped.

Splash.

They bobbed up to their chins.

"I can't believe I'm doing this. I'm so embarrassed," Julie said.

"How can you be embarrassed? You're skinnier than me." Missy floated over to the side, near the middle. "Let's do laps. We can swim back and forth and we won't see each other," She giggled.

They did a couple of laps, made up another swim routine, and were enjoying themselves when they heard a noise.

"Brrr Brbrbrbr Thwok. Brrr Brbrbr. Brrr Brbrbrbr Thwok. Brrr Brbrbr."

They froze in position, up on one foot and their arms out like wings. Julie lost balance and went under and Missy swam to her end of the pool.

Bang. The screen door slammed shut.

Tommy ran across the grass towards the pool. "Tommy, stop." He skidded to a halt on the edge of the deck.

"Did you hear it?" He threw up his arms.

"How did you know we were out here?"

"I went downstairs and you weren't there."

"Brrr Brbrbrbr Thwok. Brrr Brbrbr. Brrr Brbrbrbr Thwok. Brrr Brbrbr."

"Hear it?" He pranced in circles. "I hope the Indian Chief warrior stops the bad tractor man from digging."

"What is he talking about?" Julie grabbed her towel from the deck and wrapped it around herself, still standing in the water.

"No idea. Little kids, big imaginations. It's nothing," Missy looked at Tommy, "You go back to bed. We're getting out of the pool now. Go."

"You never believe me," he mumbled as he went back inside.

"My skinny-dipping career is over for good," Julie said as she grabbed a dry towel. Wrapping one around herself, Missy led the way back to the basement, leaving wet footprints on the carpet.

After they dressed, Julie fluffed up her beanbag. "What's Tommy talking about?" She put down her pillow, got comfy on the bag, and brought her blanket up to her chin.

"Nothing major." Missy sat on her beanbag and placed the pillow on her lap.

"It seems major to me." She looked over at Missy and waited.

"He's gotten into his head he's seen a Native Chief ghost, and the ghost Chief talked to him. He showed him where to dig up an arrowhead."

Julie sat up. "Are you serious?"

Missy could tell she was impressed. "No."

Missy didn't know if she was happy or not with other people hearing the backhoe noise, too. It had been her private nightmare for a long time. And much as she hated it, at least it wasn't bothering anyone else. Besides, her summer was ruined before it began. Life wasn't fair.

"Does this have something to do with your premonition dreams? Do the cops think it's a ghost driving the backhoe"?

"I don't want to talk." Missy placed her pillow under her head.

She could feel Julie's eyes on her for a while, but her lips were sealed and Julie gave up. They didn't talk about the Native American Chief, ghosts, or the backhoe.

***

"How many more holes Jim?" Dwight shouted as Jim chugged the backhoe to another spot on the field.

Jim helped up five fingers and crossed two for good luck. Mother Nature had been a little nicer with the fog except for one night when he started to dig, it rained. He was grateful only five rounds of dirt were lifted before it started. Mud was a messy, hard thing to dig and refill a hole.

Dwight had kept his patience with a positive attitude. He hadn't acted like he'd been sucked into an operation for nothing. Plus, he wasn't doing any of the hard work.

Of the coffins Jim had dug up, three were empty or contained items of little value. A few times he had dug in the wrong spot and brought up bones. Human bones. *Nate must have been up to something else besides grave digging.* It freaked him out but didn't stop him from digging. Jim hoped it wouldn't come back and haunt him for messing with the dead. But at the moment, he didn't care; he wanted money and the mother lode of Twist.

A few more loads of dirt were dumped to the side and Jim lifted the fifth coffin of his countdown till the end. It felt heavy and had to balance it to stop it from falling from the scoop.

This load would take time. Dwight watched as Jim turned off the backhoe. "Got a good feeling about this one. Maybe it won't be full of antique dishes and décor."

Jim jumped off the last step of the backhoe, crowbar in hand.

"This is it, Dwight, this one is the jackpot. We'll head back to Arizona with a carload of gems." Jim pried off the lock and lifted one end of the coffin. His smile turned to a frown and stopped himself from screaming profanity. More antiques. He moved a few items around and felt something soft at the bottom.

He lifted the other half of the coffin lid and grinned hugely. Sandwich-size bags were full of Twist. He estimated fifty thousand dollars worth of drugs. "Thank you, grandparents." He turned and hugged Dwight who stood frozen.

Dwight shook his head. "Wow is all I can say." He put his hand in the coffin, seized a few bags and let them fall. "I already feel drugged."

"No time to dally. We need to unload and get out of here. The rest of the machine makings should be underneath. We can't leave without the parts to continue to make it."

He stuffed his duffle bag full of Twist. Dwight did the same. Jim scoured the coffin again, thinking he must have missed something. "This can't be happening. The parts aren't here. I'm not happy. Who knows how long it will take to dig up the last four?"

Jim didn't wait for Dwight's comments. He did a half-hearted job of filling in the hole with the coffin, parked the backhoe, and drove back to the funeral home.

"Why haven't you gone in the shack?" Dwight asked as Jim parked the car.

"Nothing in there to worry about unless it's in plain sight. I'll go soon and have another look." Jim got out of his car and grabbed both duffle bags. "I'll give you a call when I'm ready for another dig."

Dwight kept glancing at the bags with a pleading look. He wanted at least a sample. Jim read his thoughts. "Hey man, we got pressure from the suppliers. I got to keep all until I talk to my parents. Don't worry, you won't leave empty-handed."

Dwight nodded and drove away.

Jim locked the door and grinned as he lay on the cot. He used the duffle bags as his pillow.

***

Julie went home at 9:00 a.m. the following day. It wasn't a great goodbye. Missy liked Julie but sometimes she was too nervous, even for her. And Missy wasn't a hero. Ally and Maura didn't hang out with Julie, only when she was with Missy.

Ally called right after Julie left. She had stayed an extra day in Sun Valley, gotten home late the night before, and wanted Missy to come over at eleven. Maura was busy, so Missy was next in line. No Maura; a-okay with Missy.

They were having a good time in the pool doing swim races and water routines until they were interrupted as Kaleb and Brandon came outside. The boys strode down the porch from the kitchen. Missy noticed Brandon had a tan. And yeah, he had a nice body, too. She hated to admit it, but Kaleb didn't look bad either. Maybe hanging around with Brandon and his good manners were rubbing off. Even Kaleb's usual attitude had taken a turn for the better.

They dropped their towels on the ground and stood a foot from the edge of the pool. Ally and Missy glanced at each other wondering what to expect.

A big splash showered them after Brandon and Kaleb cannonballed into the pool at the same time. They surfaced for air and went right into trying to mimic the girl's routines, laughing the whole time.

Fine. Missy would amend her report. They looked ridiculous and it was funny. Missy and Ally were the butts of the joke, but they were funny, and all had a laughing fit. Missy went home not too long after, feeling a bit better.

With plenty of day left, Missy took a shower and ate an early supper. Ally called again, ended up coming over, and they lay on the trampoline side by side. They talked about the pool routine Kaleb and Brandon did.

"I'm surprised the guys came out to join us. So not like Kaleb." Missy said.

"He surprises me at times too. But it's a guy thing. Feeling masculine." Ally laughed.

"I can agree."

"I think Brandon likes you."

First, Julie said it and now Ally. Missy didn't answer her as she rubbed her head back and forth against the trampoline mesh.

"I see how he looks at you." Ally sat up. "Look at your hair," she reached out and touched the end. "Zap."

Missy laughed. "I'm Static City. Yours is spiking up a little, too. You...." She stopped. "You think he likes me?"

"Brandon?"

Missy nodded.

Ally made doodles with her finger on the trampoline. "He asked for your phone number after you left today."

Missy tried to pat down her hair. "It's a surprise to me." She gave Ally a soft nudge on her head.

"Why?"

"I don't think I'm anything special."

She looked at Missy. "You have cute freckles." She crinkled her nose. "And your eyes sparkle when you smile. Makes guys melt." She nudged back. "And I'm a little jealous."

Ally's comment was a one of a kind. Why would she admit it to Missy? Maura was the gossip queen. Was Ally putting a guilt trip on Missy so she would back off? Missy hadn't even pushed the idea Brandon liked her more than he liked Ally. He was always at her house hanging around with Kaleb.

Missy bit her lower lip with a lost look. She didn't know what to think, so she got up and jumped. After a time or two, she got the big, strong, high jump, which made Ally bounce around. Missy stopped and Ally got on her feet, too. They laughed and jumped until Ally had to go home.

Chapter 25

Jim headed to the library. Ruth's comment the previous day had latched into his brain. He even dug a few more holes in the back lot of the funeral home to see if there was an opening to a tunnel entrance. No luck.

The library had to have records describing the old tunnels under Nampa. *With luck,* he thought, *there would be an old map, and, with great luck, there'd be one covering my field on the outskirts of the town.*

Jim stopped at the checkout stand and looked at the blonde librarian's name tag. He hoped her name would say she wasn't an airhead. Fran; a name with a brain.

"Can I help you?" Fran smiled sweetly as she met Jim's eyes.

"I was wondering if you had a book of maps for Nampa in the past. You know, several years ago?"

"We have a section in the basement with older books and information. You can't check them out, but there is a copy machine you can use to make copies. Ten cents a page." Fran pointed in the direction of the staircase.

"Thank you." Jim made his way to the basement. He could tell it would take him some time to find what he was looking for. He went to the computer and typed in 'Nampa old tunnels.' Several books, magazines, and maps popped up with different locations.

Great. I'll be here all day. His attitude wasn't a happy one. He took a scrap of paper and wrote some of the locations. Three of the books were in the exact location and seeing the tables were occupied with older adults he didn't want to sit by, he sat on the floor and started to search.

***

The phone rang and interrupted Missy's reading another good part in one of her favorite books. The phone had a curse on her when she got to a kissy point in the story. Not fair. "Yeah."

There was a slight pause, *"Missy?"*

She marked her page and put the book down. "Oh, hi, this is Missy."

"It's Brandon."

"Hey."

"Was wondering if you wanted to meet at the library at 11 a.m."

"Sure. Why?"

"Nampa history. I did a little research and found out the field across the street from you used to be an Indian graveyard. Was hoping to find more information.

"Seriously?"

"Yep. I can come and get you."

163

"Well, um, I'll get a ride." The last thing Missy wanted to do was tell her mom out of the blue she wanted to go to the library alone with Brandon. Her mom would say 'No'. Sometimes Missy felt like she was being raised in a pioneer lifestyle.

Missy was sure Brandon had a computer at home and could look anything up on Google. She bet Ally and or Kaleb told him Missy didn't have a cell or internet access. She would play along like they didn't even exist and go with the flow.

"Sounds good." Brandon sounded drawn back.

"OK, see you there." Missy hung up, grabbed her library card, and stuffed it in her front pocket. She didn't want to haul her wallet around in her hand or jammed in her back pocket. A glance in the mirror: no noticeable zits to pop. She also took off her hair band.

Mrs. Mack was on the couch reading. "Mom, there's not much going on and I'm kind of bored."

Missy's mom raised her eyebrows and took a deeper look at her daughter's face. "You've hardly eaten and lost some weight. Don't tell me you're starving yourself."

"No, I'm fine. Had a hard time sleeping," she shrugged. "I wanted to see if they had any new books I might like to borrow from the library."

"Are you meeting friends there?"

Missy nodded. "Yep. Can you give me a ride?"

"Sure." She got up and walked to her room. "Your dad wanted to try out a new cafe that opened downtown a couple of weeks ago." She picked up her purse. "It would give you about an hour and a half. Tommy's at his friend's the rest of the day so you wouldn't have to watch him at the library."

"Thank you."

***

"I'll be back around 12:30 PM," Mrs. Mack said, as Missy got out of the car and closed the door.

She waved, watched her mom drive off and looked around the street, and didn't see Brandon's truck. *What if he changed his mind?*

She entered the reading area near the main entrance and waited. The left wall was full of old pictures of Nampa. The Snake River Stampede, horses with riders, bull riders getting bucked off, and the clowns running around to distract the bull when the rider fell. Pictures of the town's first hospital, the train depot, and the Dewey Palace hung on the other side of the main door. Lost in her thoughts, she didn't see Brandon come in.

"Earth to Missy," Brandon said as he placed his hand on her back.

Her body shivered. "See the Palace?" She pointed at it.

"Big. What happened?"

"They demolished it in 1963." Missy looked closer. "See the bricks?"

"Yeah," Brandon replied.

"We have some. They dumped the bricks and debris in the dirt pit." She smiled. "My dad hauled out several pieces and used them for landscaping in our backyard."

"Cool." Brandon took her hand with ease. The same tingle feeling was there, and Missy wondered if Brandon felt it, too. She liked it. She took a firm hold and led the way to the history section in the basement.

***

Jim found the paper reporting his accident and "death" at the pit. It didn't make for pleasant reading. It brought the whole incident back and made his shoulder ache. He stopped reading and put the paper down. He needed a break. Looking around, standing by the computer was the girl he had kept from falling under people's feet at the Parade. She stood next to a kid he'd seen jog at night when he drove to the shack. The boy reminded Jim of a "neighborhood watchdog", and didn't like it. He raised an eyebrow when he saw they were holding hands.

He finished reading the article, and then massaged his forehead. Going through the whole grim story gave him a migraine, which didn't improve his mood. *My history,* Jim thought. *Nothing's going to change it.*

The kids moved to a section on the other end, away from Jim. He went back to one of the three computers and wrote down more locations to search.

He heard a muffled conversation and noticed the two teens had moved to the next aisle across from him. Jim got bits of their conversation, the books being a good sound buffer.

"Native American, history, pit, ghosts."

They were interested in a little ghost hunting. No matter. They weren't going to get in his way. He closed the book and fitted it back onto the shelf. Jim eased down the aisle in the opposite direction from where the kids were standing. He didn't want to attract attention. He listened.

***

"Here, take this," Brandon handed Missy a book.

She turned the pages, scanning the title. "Idaho's History of Native American Tribes."

"I hope it's a good one." He flipped through another book as they sat at a table by the computers.

"I can't find anything on Native American or a graveyard." Missy flipped back through the different sections: *Old Town Nampa. Tunnels. Whoa. This is better.* "Now we're getting somewhere." She tapped her fingers on the desk.

"What?"

"Tommy came home from a field trip after meeting a Native Warrior. My little brother's got a good imagination. He told me something about a Bigfoot story. I thought he meant the Sasquatch."

Brandon nodded.

"But look at this. This Native Brave was seven feet tall and his feet were over 17 inches long. A big guy."

Missy inhaled a deep breath. "He could run for hours and he was fast. There's more. He wasn't pure Native American."

"So."

"I'm reading what it says here. I wonder how big the ghost Tommy saw was. This Brave was half-white, one-quarter African-American, and one-quarter Native." She

167

scanned to the end of the page. "Oh, my heck. Look at this."

Brandon looked on while she read it out loud. "The word for 'Bigfoot' in Native American is Nampai." Missy scratched her shoulder. "See? The town is named Nampa. Their chief was Chief Nampai." She slapped the page. "We live in Bigfoot, Idaho. Thoughts?"

"Not yet," he said. "Maybe he's our ghost, maybe not."

"But if it is him, why would he be haunting me? Or is he warning me of the person who drives the backhoe and digs in the field?"

Brandon shrugged as Missy opened another history book she got from the shelf.

"We need to know more. Hey, look at this." She pointed at a picture of a small doll. "I've seen this picture before. This is the Nampa Image Doll."

Brandon gave her a puzzled look and shook his head.

"You're new to Nampa. Anyhow, this doll was found in 1889 when some men were digging a well."

"For water?"

"Uh-huh. Says here they dug through 320 feet of lava and clay when they found it. Now it's in the Boise Museum."

"Three hundred and twenty feet? Very deep."

"It's what it says in the book," She shrugged.

"Nice. Let's keep reading."

Missy found the information interesting but figured Brandon was more into sports. Maybe she should research Football and become a Boise State Broncos fan.

She got up and followed the History in Idaho section into the next aisle. For a small city, they had a good-sized collection of books. There was one on the Sugar Factory. *Maybe it says how to deal with the disgusting smell when they ran the machines. The whole town stank.*

There were books on politics, Native American rights, North America during the Ice Age, but nothing Brandon or Missy needed.

She kept going. She walked to the other side of the long bookshelf and found a pile of old newspapers stacked in order on a shelf. She had a hunch she'd find something, gathered the pile, and took them back to their table.

Nothing special. Life as usual in Nampa, except the advertisements weren't on the front page anymore. She kept searching and reached 1990. Missy knew her mom graduated the same year.

Holy smoke.

"Hey." Missy shoved the paper under Brandon's face. "Look at this."

The headline took up three columns on the bottom half of the front page.

TRACTOR RACE LEADS TO DEATH
1989 HIGH SCHOOL GRADUATE
JAMES FORST MEETS A TRAGIC END
ANOTHER GHOST IN THE MISTY FIELD?
Nampa Gravel Pit

"Another year to celebrate Idaho Potatoes. The tractor race caused the death…. the catastrophe, will this accident stop the yearly Potato Races?

James "Jim" Forst ran into some complications with his tractor. "It seemed to lose control," Raymond Mack, a witness of the tragedy said, "Jim tried to stop his tractor before it crashed into the pit."

"This tragedy affects the town. We have lost a student, a friend, and a community member. A family of Nampa has lost their only son.

A closed casket funeral and a private service will be held for immediate family. The cause of the accident is still under investigation."

There were a couple of side stories, students at the scene of the accident who were interviewed, a brief history of the pit, and a short piece about how Jim's parents were so distraught, they left Nampa for good.

"No do you believe in the rumors of ghosts at the pit and my dreams?" Missy did a mental head slap. *Crap. I don't want Brandon to know about my dreams yet or never.*

"Dreams?" He scratched his head.

"Never mind."

"Do you know who this Jim guy was?"

"I know a little. He was my mom's boyfriend in high school for a while. They didn't interview her." Missy said. "The tractor in the pit is the same one he died in. The police left it there as a reminder. You know: like the car accident on the side-of-the-road warning. There were no more tractor races and the pit is full of junk now. Maybe he's the ghost, driving the backhoe?"

Brandon shrugged. "Why didn't you use this for your writing assignment?"

Missy was clueless for a good answer, so she changed the subject. "The way I've heard it before the pit turned into a junk collector, it was a quarry for a while. They dug up the boulders and rocks at the pit to grind them for gravel road filler. One morning, when the workers got there, they saw a mist on the field. People said it was because of the lake." Missy sat back. "But the men who were working in the pit swear they saw spirits or ghosts floating around who looked angry."

Brandon continued where she left off. "Floating spirits, oh boy. Whatever. Let's suppose it's Jim and he's alive. If it's possible. I mean if he's alive, he's come back for something." Excited, his voice rose. Two older ladies who showed up a few minutes before at the computer tossed disgusted looks in their direction.

Missy smiled at the ladies, winked the "boys will be boys" look and turned back to Brandon. "It can't be Jim. He's dead. According to the article, he was, uh, you know." She made a motion with her hands; crushed. "The police had an awful time getting his body out, and spirits don't drive backhoes." *Or do they? I mean, seriously. Is Jim alive?* "He couldn't be alive." Missy looked at Brandon. *If he'd been saved, it would have been a medical miracle and big news. But peeved-off Native spirits? Interesting. A definite maybe.*

"What do you mean?"

"Out of luck," *I'm not going to tell Brandon I eves-dropped.* "I heard my mom telling my dad she saw someone who

171

looked like Jim at the store. But everyone has a twin, right? You know, someone who looks like you. That was before I saw him and my mom together in her yearbook. Mom said he got in an accident and died." She folded the newspaper and put it back in the pile. "Time for some tunnel research."

Brandon nodded. They looked at more books on the computer.

***

Those kids are snooping and going places they shouldn't go. Jim swore in his mind and had heard enough. He double-checked no one was looking and came around to the table where the stack of Nampa papers lay. Taking great care, he tore out the cover story, turned to page three, and did the same. He folded the old columns of newspaper in half, avoiding making a hard crease, and looked to see if he was clear to leave.

Jim peeked around the back shelf and saw the kids coming back. He squatted to pretend to look at the bottom shelf of books and got in earshot of Missy and Brandon talking again.

***

"But what if he didn't die?" Brandon asked. "What if it was a cover-up and now he's back for a reason?"

A cold breeze blew by and ruffled Missy's bangs and Brandon's loose-fitting shirt. They both looked to see if there was a window. There wasn't. Goosebumps popped up on Missy's arms.

172

"Do you see a fan running?" Brandon looked around and at the ceiling.

Missy didn't see anyone walk by them and followed suit on any fans running. "That was freaky. Maybe it was the chief trying to warn us?"

"I'm not sure I want to know. Overall, I know we are looking into places we should leave alone." Brandon rested his chin on his palms.

"Let's suppose you're correct," Missy ignored Brandon's statement. "When did the race occur?"

Brandon and Missy headed to the table where the newspapers were stacked. She didn't know what they were looking for now, but something. Anything.

She went back to the original newspaper where the accident was posted. "It's gone."

"What's gone?"

"Someone ripped out the article. And look," She turned to page three. "The rest of it's gone, too. But it was here."

"Maybe you've got the wrong day. And people, they shouldn't, but they do rip out pages. I'll help you. We'll go through the stack and find it."

Five minutes later, after the whole stack was searched, they came up empty-handed. "It's gone. We can tell the librarian, but what can she do? See if the info is on google? But it's history."

They went to the librarian's desk. A sign was there saying if you need help, go to the main floor.

"We can call later, or come back, but unless there are microfiche or newspaper copies…" Missy looked at the clock on the wall. "Crap, it is 12:30. My mom will be here any second."

***

Jim didn't like the fact two teens were trying to be detectives. They were reading about him and now thought he could be a ghost. In reality, Jim was. He was stuck and couldn't find anything about the tunnels. He was ready to leave. He couldn't wait any longer. The day was wasted.

He looked at the floor as he passed the kids and jogged up the stairs. When he reached the main floor, a loud voice bellowed out of the speakers, "The library is now on a mandatory lockdown. Please stay inside, be patient, and we'll keep you informed."

Jim didn't care and jogged out into the street without checking traffic.

Tires squealed. A car horn blasted. He gave a glance and kept going. *A lady driver, as usual. They don't watch where they are going. They were too busy fixing their lipstick or texting to the lady's gossip club. Or she was a mad driver and caused the library to go into lockdown.*

He didn't give the driver a second glance and continued running as fast as he could until he reached his car and was inside. *What a stupid move,* he thought. *I've got to be careful. I almost caused myself to be a ghost. For real. And what a waste it would be. A waste of a fortune in drugs.* He chuckled nervously and drove back to the funeral home.

***

Missy and Brandon stood by the stairs. "Now what? My mom's out there freaking out."

"You can use my cell." Brandon handed it to her.

"Thanks." Missy dialed her mom's number.

"Hi, Mom?"

What's going on? I see police cars and ambulances all over the street a block from the library. They're directing traffic away and I can't wait any longer.

"We were told it's a mandatory lockdown in the library until further notice."

I'm worried, plus I almost hit a guy who ran out of the library's door. He didn't even look.

A librarian worker passed by and told people there had been shooting close by.

"Just notified there is a shooting in the area."

How are you going to get home? I'm told to leave.

"I got a ride."

Who?

"Brandon." Missy heard her mom sigh as Brandon nodded on the ride.

Be careful and call me on any updates. I have to run to Boise and can't get ahold of your dad.

"I will, and love you."

Missy and Brandon took their time waiting and found some books that had more info about the tunnels. Forty-five minutes later, they were allowed to leave. The coast was clear.

***

Jim parked his car at the funeral home and discovered he was still a little spooked. Being run down in traffic would not be a good thing. He had come too close for comfort. Jim heard some person yell as he ran out the library's door, 'Careful, there's a shooter out there.' He was under enough stress as it was.

Jim took out a small bit of a downer drug to calm himself. He made his way to a thrift store and got a cheap picture frame. He preferred something nicer but it had to be 'second hand.' His supply of money, both real and fake, was limited now, but he hoped not for long. He dropped the frame off in his car and headed to The Red Steer for a meal and a drink.

Chapter 26

"You want to stop at Dairy King?" Brandon asked as they got into his truck after leaving the library.

"I guess."

He saw Missy dig into her pocket feeling for change, "I got it," he smiled.

Melt City. "Thank you." She glanced out the window as they drove away, feeling good and nervous as heck at the same time. *Is this how you feel when you like someone? Not that I haven't liked other boys, but it feels different with Brandon.*

They drove to the Dairy King, found a spot close to the door, and parked. Brandon opened the car door for Missy like a perfect gentleman, and held the shop door, too.

I could get used to this star treatment. She smiled as they went inside.

Brandon glanced around. "No crowd, no lines. What do you like?"

"Peanut Parfait."

He ordered at the counter. "I'd like one Peanut Parfait and a banana split."

"Anything else?" the clerked asked. Brandon looked at Missy who shook her head.

"Nah, I'm good."

"Seven dollars and twenty-four cents, please."

Brandon counted out the money from his pocket and handed it to the clerk. The clerk gave him a receipt. He led Missy to a bench in the back. Missy scooted in, and Brandon sat across from her. "You seem quiet."

"I'm thinking."

He nodded.

"Number forty-five." Their order was done.

Missy started to stand up, but Brandon continued to be a gentleman. "Stay put. I'll get it." He brought back the two orders and placed Missy's in front of her. Picking up his spoon and arranging a bite, a little banana, whipped cream and nuts, he asked, "Are you scared of tripping into me again?"

Another surprise comment from Brandon, and Missy wasn't sure how to handle it. She put her spoon down. "Yes," then paused. "And this whole thing with the pit and spirits, it's creeping me out. Not to mention someone tore the article out of the paper while we weren't looking. I hear the backhoe out there more often now. It used to be twice a month, and it's happening more often. I want a break from the darn thing. No one should be out there. The field isn't used for farming anymore. What is the backhoe doing, riding around in the dead of the night? Who's driving it?" Missy realized her voice had raised and she tried to mellow out.

"Sorry." Brandon took a mouthful of ice cream.

She looked around to see if anyone was listening in. "No prob. I'm tired of not sleeping. It gives me nightmares. My parents don't know. I don't want to worry them." Missy took a bite of her parfait and let it slither down her throat. *Crap, I'm saying too much to a person I'm trying to impress.*

"Here." Brandon wiped her chin. "You had a little chocolate there."

Missy felt like throwing the spoon and banging her head on the table, but she didn't. *First, I trip on the bus and at the parade. I'm a klutz. Now I'm messy when I eat my food. Could it get any worse?* She placed the spoon in the container and shoved it to the side. She had lost her appetite.

Brandon looked at her but kept his mouth buttoned. Missy was glad he didn't push it, and ended up taking a couple more bites of her parfait to let him know she was fine, then let him finish his treat in peace. They got into his truck and drove to his house.

Missy knew she liked Brandon a lot and hoped he didn't think she was kind of a freaked-out nerd. She felt uncomfortable by the time they got to his house. *I thought he was taking me home. Uh-oh.* A look at the dashboard's clock told her differently. *2:00 p.m. Plenty of time to waste until 3:00 p.m.*

Brandon put the truck in park and turned off the engine. "You seem extra quiet."

Missy's stomach did its knot tying episode. Pressing the seatbelt release, she looked over at him. He placed his hand in hers, "It's going to be fine. I'll do what I can to help you figure out the backhoe."

She gave him a small smile.

He climbed out and made it to the passenger's side in time to open the door for Missy. She wasn't sure if she could take this right now.

They got inside the foyer and Brandon stopped. "FYI, my mom is a no-shoe-in-the-house person. My parents lived in Japan for a while and she liked the custom." He removed his shoes and set them by the wall. Missy did the same with her sandals.

"I heard that, Brandon," a female voice called out from the kitchen.

He smiled, shrugged, and gestured for Missy to follow him.

"Hi, Mom."

"Hello, yourself. This must be Melissa." Brandon's mom offered her hand. "I'm Rita Miller and you can call me Rita."

"Hi. Something smells good." She mentally slapped her forehead. *The things I say and do. Argh.*

Brandon raised his eyebrows.

Mrs. Miller led them into the kitchen. "Those are my specialty: cinnamon oatmeal cookies." She looked through the glass oven door. "Give it five more minutes. Brandon said you might be coming over today. Treats are a must for visitors at our home."

"Happy times," Missy said.

"You're always welcome to visit." She washed her hands in the kitchen sink. "Brandon, could you please get out mugs and napkins."

"Okay."

Missy followed Brandon to the cupboard, handed her a cup and got two more.

"The reward for cooking is to eat what I make," Brandon's mom said.

They watched, quiet and comfortable, for a few minutes. The timer buzzed. Brandon's mom slipped on the mitts, opened the oven door, and got the hot cookie tray out. "Perfect." The aroma was cinnamon heaven.

They waited at the table while Brandon's mom took the cookies off the tray and placed them on a cooling rack. "Don't burn your mouths. I made them for you to eat, I'll get the milk." She placed the rack on the table.

There they were. Nice as you please. They ate the cookies right off the cooling rack. Way cool. Brandon's mom sat across from them. She was attractive, with shoulder-length sandy blond hair. Missy thought she could be a petite model.

"What do your parents do for work?" she asked
Missy.

Missy took a big gulp of milk. "First off, these cookies are a knockout."

"Knockout, eh? Brandon and his father tell me 'good' or 'great', but a knockout? I'll keep it in mind." Mrs. Miller snickered.

"My dad is an accountant. He works for the town. My mom sometimes helps him but she's also a stay-at-home mom because I have a little brother, Tommy. Do you work?"

Brandon's mom wiped her lips daintily with the napkin. "I have lots of jobs: Nurse, accountant, electrical engineer, plumber, carpenter, and maid. Now, this was a hard decision, but I of late, retired as the family taxi driver." She nodded towards Brandon who rolled his eyes. "He's the new taxi driver in the family since he has his license."

They both laughed, and Missy joined in.

They had another round of cookies. "What does your husband do?"

"He travels a lot. Has to go to a lot of meetings."

Missy raised her eyebrows, inquiring.

Brandon and Mrs. Miller looked at each other, nodded, and she looked back to Missy. "He's in, mmm, research."

Missy was clueless. She couldn't place Brandon's dad as a person to call strangers on the phone and ask countless stupid questions.

"The other way of saying it is he's a DEA," Brandon said.

"A what?" Missy adjusted herself in the chair and felt Brandon's hand touch hers for a quick second.

"It stands for Drug Enforcement Agent."

Missy tried to hold back her emotions. "Does he have to find bad people?" The question came out in a higher pitch.

Mrs. Miller nodded. "He does, but I've got things to do around the house. You two finish off the cookies and give me a shout if you need anything." She got up, pushed her chair in, and left the kitchen. They were alone.

"Your mom's nice."

"Yeah, she's all right."

"You have any brothers or sisters?"

"A brother. He's in college."

"Cool."

"Feeling any better?"

Missy nodded. He touched her shoulder for a few seconds and moved it back to his lap. The electric buzz she felt turned off. Phew.

"Talking to your mom and eating these cookies helped. Sorry for wasting the Peanut Parfait." She looked around trying to find a clock. No luck, but the time was done for Missy. "I need to get home. I'll see you later?" *Me and my stupid questions.*

"I can walk with you," he offered as she headed to the front door.

He rested against the door as Missy slipped on her sandals. "It was a nice visit, but I can make it home fine by myself."

He gave a single nod and opened the door for her. "See you soon."

"Okay." *Maybe he did want to see me.*

The five-minute walk home seemed to take five hours. Missy's thoughts were one big mess. Having a new person in her life wasn't easy.

***

Brandon went back to the table, go the mugs and napkins, and placed the dirty dishes in the kitchen sink as his mom came in. "Why the miserable look?"

He turned to her. "How long are we going to be here?"

"What do you mean?"

Brandon propped back against the counter and folded his arms. "When Dad finishes this job he's on, are we moving again? I'm tired of moving." He looked at his feet.

She reached behind and rubbed his back. "I know it's hard at your age. You make friends, and we end up moving."

"True."

"You like Melissa, don't you?"

He lifted his head. "I guess."

"We're going to be here for a long time. Your father promised me." She smiled. "Don't you go and worry, 'k?" She kissed his cheek and left him standing alone. Allowing himself a small smile, he gave the counter a victorious pat and went to his room.

***

Depression had hit Missy before, but not as bad as today. She got home from Brandon's and went straight to her room to read a book to clear her mind. It had been a busy week and she was on her second book.

At least her appetite was back some. Missy managed to eat a little at dinner. *Mom's been watching over me like I was a sick kitten.* Both her parents were full of questions. "How is the library?" "What was it like at Brandon's house?" "Did she like Brandon's mom?" "What did Brandon's father do?" Missy did her best to answer but had to get away. She excused herself and went back to bed.

Julie was a phone call away, but Missy didn't feel like talking. With her luck, Julie wouldn't want to talk to her. Missy's mom came into her room around 8:00 p.m. She sat on the side of her bed. "Are you feeling sick again?"

"You keep asking me like a thousand times a day. I'm fine."

"Did Brandon say something to hurt you?"

"No. I'm tired."

She felt Missy's forehead and ears. "You don't feel warm. A little too much running around, I bet." She patted her leg. "You get a good night's rest."

Missy turned over onto her side and faced the wall. She didn't feel like talking or listening. Her mom closed the door and left Missy alone.

Chapter 27

Jim took a last big gulp of his Pepsi and tossed the can in the trash. He had felt his cell phone buzz a minute earlier but didn't want to answer it. The number was unrecognizable, but knew who it was. Jim was sure Carlos was calling to put the pressure on even more. He put the cell on speaker and listened to the voicemail.

"Yo, Jimmy. What's taking you so long? Ha, ha. The deadline is next week, man. I'm tired and my patience is growing thin. You come across with those parts soon or your contract will expire, too. Ha ha." Click.

Carlos. Fun guy. He had been tolerable in the beginning, but now things were getting serious. Jim liked the guy as much as he could. This deal with the drugs should have been easy pickings, but no. His grandparents had done too good a job and it made his life complicated. He grabbed a hammer and a handful of nails. Time for an up-to-date decoration in the shack.

***

Jim sat on the cot and adjusted himself for comfort despite the lack of padding. He admired the newspaper article framed in the middle of the wall opposite. It read:

TRACTOR RACE LEADS TO DEATH
1989 HIGH SCHOOL GRADUATE
JAMES FORST MEETS A TRAGIC END
ANOTHER GHOST IN THE MISTY FIELD?
Nampa Gravel Pit

"Another year to celebrate Idaho Potatoes. The tractor race caused the death.... the catastrophe, will this accident stop the yearly Potato Races?

James "Jim" Forst ran into some complications with his tractor. "It seemed to lose control," Raymond Mack, a witness of the tragedy said, "Jim tried to stop his tractor before it crashed down into the pit."

"Celebrating Idaho potatoes," Jim said to nobody. *Boy, do those guys know how to lay it on.* He read on.

"Ray tried to stop my tractor from crashing into the pit? Hah. Nice whitewash. It was a dirty race from the beginning." Jim knew he talked to the wall, but the wall was the only thing listening.

He remembered Ray trying to stay ahead of him. *No one gets by Jim Forst. No one. Imagine Violet was going to replace him with Raymond Mack? Hah. What a laugh. I should have won the stupid race. If it wasn't for the rock sticking out at the edge of the pit, it would have been Ray rolling down the edge, not me.*

If it wasn't for the rock, the whole race would have turned out another way, and a few dirty cops on the payroll helped. Nothing like money to shut a person up. If I could've jumped, all would have been fine, but the big pile of soft dirt saved me or I would have been flattened like a pancake. Mack ruined my shoulder and my life.

Jim was grateful his family had a couple of contacts in the Nampa upper class. His uncle, who had passed away a few years ago, was the doctor who confirmed Jim's death. He had set up a surgery with his contacts in Arizona to work on Jim's shoulder. His uncle took care of the funeral arrangements with his connections and all was fine. People came to a funeral with an empty casket.

Jim smacked his hand on the dark blue camp blanket. *Time to find my drug stash and get the heck out of this place.* He'd had his fill of Nampa.

The framed newspaper article added a little color to the dull room. He removed the photograph of Violet out of his wallet. Jim looked at it with remorse. She was sixteen and beautiful. The camera had captured the mischievous look in her eyes. It added to what made her attractive. Jim remembered the teenybopper who tripped into him at the parade the other day and had seen her at the library. Sitting with one of the "Hardy Boys", no doubt. Jim realized Violet and the girl looked like twins. No mistake. This girl had to be Violet's daughter. He ran his thumb over Violet's face in the photograph and remembered how soft her skin was. Her hair, her touch.

Jim was tempted to do something ugly: Stomp on the photograph, tear it into little pieces, or burn it. Instead, he calmed himself and stuck the picture on the bottom corner of the frame. He liked looking at Violet's, even though the time for remembering such feelings had passed. He felt the pressure from Carlos and knew the next conversation wouldn't finish with a laugh.

The old metal gas tank for the backhoe sat next to the table with a nice smell. Jim held the rusty cap tight and turned. A piece of metal on the cap dented out and cut his finger on the turn and tossed the cap. It bounced under the cot behind him.

"Well, isn't life just peachy." He sucked on his finger and went to pick up the cap. He moved the cot away from the wall and bent over to grab it and noticed the floor had a small opening.

"What in the heck?"

Jim took the hammer from the table, set the claws in the crack, and gave the hammer a good yank. A crack beneath the board was exposed.

"What have we got here?" Jim asked the air around him. He tossed the hammer aside and heaved the loose board up. Jim seized his flashlight, got on his stomach, and aimed the beam of light into the hollow.

Jim cursed at himself. *Stupid, stupid, stupid. And downright lazy. But on the other hand, funny. Forget the backhoe and digging like a field-hand ghost. I found a tunnel. Money and the Twist-making machine parts had to be there.*

Chapter 28

Mrs. Mack checked on Missy again before she went to bed. "Want me to get you anything to eat? Crackers, soup, ice-cream?" She found Missy sitting up, reading.

"No, I'm fine. If I feel worse, I'll let you know." Missy forced a smile.

Her mom nodded and left whispering loud enough for Missy to hear two of the words, "Need counseling."

Do I look like I'm bad enough for counseling? Even a psychiatrist wouldn't understand how I feel. They'd only want to put me on drugs. Missy had finished her book and tried to read another one to stay awake. Her nightmares had gotten more confusing and dangerous. She got to page 10 before the book fell out of her hands as she went to sleep.

It was a hot day, and Missy wanted to float in the ditch on her homemade raft. She called her friends and asked them to come with her. They all said the same. "Sorry, Missy. Busy." Too bad for them; she'd go by herself.

With her rolled-up pant legs, a straw hat, and a piece of grass between her teeth, she made it to the top of the field with her raft and placed it in the water.

Missy situated herself in the middle of the raft and, with a thick branch she'd found, pushed off the side of the ditch. The ride was nice and smooth. She reached the tree with the rope hanging still out of reach and could imagine the echoes of her and her friends laughing and screaming. It brought a smile to her face.

The shack loomed in the distance. As Missy neared it, the raft bounced, like an unbalanced washer. She stared into the water. It was crystal clear and as smooth as glass. 'You have one heck of an imagination, Missy.' Maybe it's the sun. She had forgotten to put on sunscreen.

The raft gained speed. Missy fell, grabbed the boards, and held on for her life. Something in the water jolted her, and the raft bucked, to the right and to the left, over and over. Her grip grew weak.

The raft spun. Missy clung with all her strength, air whizzing in her face, as it went airborne. She fell hard into the water beneath the upturned raft. She needed to get her head above water before she drowned. Missy couldn't push the raft away. She was trapped. Something knocked her on the forehead hard. If she was going to drown, she would give one more chance to survive.

Missy kicked, moved, and screamed to get out from under the raft. Her forehead hurt from hitting the wood time after time again to try to break it up.

More pressure weighed on Missy making it harder to maneuver. She took her last breath, relaxed her body and let go of the raft.

She heard her guardian angels call out for her to join them in heaven. "Missy, Missy come out of it. Wake up. Missy! *Missy!!!*"

Mrs. Mack tried to untangle Missy from her blankets and sheet.

Missy gasped for air.

"Sweetie, you're fine." She cuddled her daughter. Missy clung to her for all she was worth. "Another bad dream?"

Missy nodded. "How do you know?

"I've heard you tossing and turning and grunting off and on for weeks. But it seems to be an almost nightly trauma. Want to talk about it?"

"No. Nothing major."

"It must be major. You hardly eat or do things with your friends. Something is bugging you. Want to go see a counselor?"

"Can I just go back to sleep, please? I'm tired."

Missy's mom kissed her forehead and tucked her back in bed. "I'm sorry for questioning you but your dad and I are worried." She closed the door quietly.

Missy nodded, fell back to sleep, and back into another dream.

"I promise, Julie. This is the last time we will go into the pit. I want to see the old tractor. I promise."

"Every time I follow along to what you say, I get hurt. I'm starting to catch up with you being a klutz." She gave Missy a dirty look.

"One last time. Nothing's going to happen I promise." Missy took Julie's arm and steered her to the edge of the Pit. "The hill isn't steep to climb down." She took the first step.

"Here, let me go first. Then I can stop you from falling if you decided to trip." Julie sounded sarcastic.

"I don't want to knock you over. I should go first."

"Whatever," Julie said. She went ahead and stepped in front of Missy.

Bad choice. After five steps, Julie tripped, fell, and didn't stop. The bottom of the pit was an open black hole.

Missy kicked the wall by her bed. "Help, Help. Julie fell. Help!" She screamed. "I can't stop her."

***

Mr. and Mrs. Mack ran into Missy's room and turned on the light. Missy kicked the wall again and wrestled around on her bed like fighting a snake. Missy's dad grabbed her legs as her mom sat on the side of the bed and put her arms over her body to calm her down.

"Missy. Wake up Missy," Her mom said.

She moved to her back, opened her eyes and stared off to the unknown.

Tommy came into the room with a confused look. "What happened?"

"Bad dream. Got back to bed please," Mr. Mack said. Tommy shrugged and left.

Mr. and Mrs. Mack let go of Missy but stayed in place if another attack happened. If Missy wasn't breathing, she'd pass as a ghost. Her eyes dilated. She was shriving as if she was in an ice freezer, but beads of sweat rolled down her face.

"I'm going to take her to ER It looked like she had a seizure," Mrs. Mack looked at her husband as she turned her daughter's head to the side to play it safe and prevent any choking. "Missy needs help. She hardly eats and I hope it's not the start of anorexia. That causes seizures."

193

Mr. Mack got a pair of socks out of Missy's drawer. "Funny business is going on with drugs and the digging in the field. It seems right at the end of school Missy's started being more depressed." He put the socks on Missy's feet. She hadn't moved.

"What about Brandon? You've told me Missy likes him. I hope he's not causing the trouble." Missy's dad helped his wife sit Missy up and put on some sweats.

Mrs. Mack shook Missy's shoulders to get a response. "I hope not, too." They helped Missy stand and Mr. Mack expressed a concerned look. "By the time we call an ambulance and they arrive, I'll be in the ER Room. I believe Missy's more tired and lack of nutrition than in shock." They walked Missy to the car and got her situated in the front seat. "I'll give you a call if they will want to keep her overnight."

Mr. Mack nodded and went inside.

***

They placed Missy into an ER room on arrival and administered an I.V. Mrs. Mack told the Doctor about Missy's continuous nightmares and not eating much, and longer periods of depression besides the normal once a month cycle.

Two hours later, with a prescription of sleeping pills and a list of counselors to contact, Mrs. Mack got home and, with Mr. Mack's help, put Missy to bed. Her color had returned some and her eyes were clearer.

Mrs. Mack placed her hand on Missy's arm. She was half asleep with the medicine given to her at ER "I'm sorry mom. I."

She put her finger on Missy's lip. "Shhh. You have nothing to worry about. Go to sleep. You'll be fine." She raised the blanket up to Missy's chin. "Goodnight." Missy had fallen back to sleep.

Missy's dad stood by her bedroom door as his wife ran her fingers through Missy's hair. "She's at peace now." Mrs. Mack walked over and rested on Mr. Mack's shoulder. "I hope so. Summer is the fun time of the year for kids. I might have to ask around about Brandon and if anyone knows more about him than Missy thinks she does."

They took one more look at their daughter and went to their bedroom. "Remember me telling you about Missy asking who Jim was when she looked at my yearbook?"

Mr. Mack nodded.

"Maybe she heard me telling you I saw a look-a-like. Maybe she's seen this person and it's scaring her. I'm not

195

sure why it would. But the noise in the field is happening more often than it has for years." Mrs. Mack put on her nightgown. "But I don't understand why it would give her nightmares." She sat on her side of the bed. "I'll look through the list of counselors tomorrow."

Chapter 29

Missy felt her body jumping around. "Missy, wake up, wake up. Cartoons are on." Tommy leaped on Missy's bed and bounced. "You're gonna miss your favorite."

Missy rolled over and covered herself again. "Stop bouncing. Leave me alone."

"It's Sponge Bob. Come on." He bounced once more.

"No. Go. Let me sleep."

Tommy jumped off the bed and stomped on the floor. "You're no fun." And slammed the door shut.

Missy didn't care and looked at her clock: 8:00 a.m. She didn't sleep most of the night and barely remembered going to the hospital.

The next time she looked at her clock it was 10:30 am. Yikes. She sprang up in bed. *I got to call Julie.* The raft was the first bad dream. The second one about Julie was worse. *I need to talk to her.*

She sat with her hand on the phone with a slight remaining lag of sleeping pills. *If I got a phone call from a friend saying they dreamed of me falling and possibly dying, would I want to hear about it?*

197

"Hi, Julie." Missy yawned into the receiver.

"Hey."

"Want to meet?"

"I guess. Where?" Julie didn't sound enthusiastic.

I'm sure Julie's thinking 'Whenever I go out with Missy, I get into danger.' "The pit in an hour."

"Sound good, bye."

"Bye."

One item done to cross off Missy's list of have-tos. The second was a shower and food. She hadn't eaten much the day before, but now starvation attacked her stomach. Sometimes, bad dreams made her hate the sight of food; sometimes she felt starved after spending a night wrestling with tractor teeth. The whole week had been crazy. The worst part was feeling like the third wheel.

Missy found her mom in the kitchen doing the dishes. "Mom, I'm meeting with Julie for a minute."

"You're up. How are you feeling?" She hugged Missy.

"Still a little tired but fine."

"Did you stay asleep after we got home?"

"Yes. I don't want to talk about it." She grabbed a piece of bread and went back to her room.

Though it was still Summer, Missy felt chilled even after her shower, so she put on her mom's 4-H jacket and hiked down the trail into the pit. Julie had beaten her there and was sitting on the mattress with her hands together on her lap. She didn't look to notice Missy. *Uh-oh. not good.*

She sat at the far end of the mattress. "Hey."

"Hey." Julie looked at the jacket Missy had on. "Cold?"

Missy rubbed her hands together, "A little." She readied herself to spill the speech she had practiced on the walk to the pit. She drew a breath. "I must have done something to upset you. Whatever it is, I'm sorry. I know you have other friends, but I thought we were sort of becoming best friends?" *I hope I don't have to bring up my visit to the hospital. Julie would for sure think I'd have to go to a mental house.*

Julie fidgeted her fingers.

"Please, Julie. Please tell me."

"Well," she looked at Missy. "You've changed."

Crap. "How?"

Julie shrugged. "I can't explain."

"Yes, you can." Missy touched her arm. "Please. I miss my best buddy."

"You're not going to like it."

Maybe not. "Shoot."

"First off, the way Maura and Ally control you like Play-Dough. It's pathetic. And to top it off, since Brandon moved here, you're far away."

"No."

"Yes." She looked at Missy with concern, picked up a rock and threw it. It clanged against another rock and stopped. "They have you in a tight knot around their finger.

"Not nice."

"More like point-blank mean. They both use you and you let them. Why?"

199

Missy shrugged. "Don't know."

"You have to stand up for yourself." Julie threw another rock. "And this backhoe stuff. Right before school got out; you weren't sleeping at night because of nightmares. The ghost we saw in this pit." She pointed up to the crashed tractor. "What are you, possessed? I don't know what to make of it. You want to be friends with *those two*, fine, but where does it leave me?" She raised her hands.

"Sorry."

"With them, you never have time for me."

"You were always riding horses. I don't have a horse. If Maura or Ally called, I'd go." Missy looked at Julie, a bit defensively.

"Maura rides her horse more than I do. I've only seen you once on their horse. But I guess it was when Ally wasn't available."

She got it right on that comment. "I thought you were tired of being friends with me."

"After you took me to this disgusting pit in the middle of the night, I was."

"You still think I did it on purpose?"

Julie nodded. "A tiny bit." She adjusted herself on the mattress and faced Missy. "I'm a chicken."

"Bbbbuuuuckkkk. Bbbbbuuuuckkkk."

A slow smile spread across Julie's face.

Missy tucked her hands under her armpits and flapped her wings.

"I got it," Julie flapped back. "We're even."

"We're both chicken."

"True." A minute or two later Julie said, "Are you and Brandon getting serious?"

"I don't know. I like him. But after our date, he's apt not to like me back."

"What do you mean?"

"I felt weird at the library. Like someone was watching me. Then we get locked in because some nut a block away was running around with a gun. Then at Dairy King, I slopped my dessert down my chin. Embarrassing. Then meeting his mom." Missy looked at the tractor. "I know he's being nice to me, but I don't know why. It's got to be a temporary thing until he finds someone better."

"I promise it will work out, and lucky for Brandon to have someone like you. And I'm sure it won't be competition even though it's confusing who is after Brandon, Maura, or Ally. But I think if Maura knows there's no chance for her, she'll take total reward in doing her best to get Ally with Brandon."

"True. Hard to believe he's interested in me and not either of them." Missy snorted.

"It's not hard to believe. Those two are plastic. He likes you. You're real."

Julie's comment made Missy smile. She felt as though it might be safe to brighten up a bit.

"Now," Julie said with authority, "tell me what this backhoe stuff is."

"I haven't told anyone. How much do you want to know?"

"Deep detail."

Missy took a breath and let it out. "Remember, we're friends."

"I'll remember."

"Where should I start?"

"The nightmares," Julie sounded certain.

"My nightmares..." Missy told her from the beginning. It took a while, and at the last, she said, "To top it off, I have other bad dreams. It's not good, Julie. Not good."

"Bad dreams are common. I have one at times, too."

"But mine aren't always dreams. It happens while I'm awake, too. Remember?"

"Yes, I remember you telling me a few weeks ago. Still wasn't sure if I believed it or not."

"Do you know?" Missy's fist hit the mattress. "Someone is digging at night looking for something, and I need to find out what it is, but I'm frightened."

"I do, and I'd be frightened, too. And I'll tell you something else: I'm never coming back to this pit at night. Never."

Missy stood. "While it's daylight, let's go see." She gestured towards the beat-up tractor.

"You've got to be kidding."

"No. Maybe it's mice. They're safe."

"I don't know what to think. If we're going to look, let's go look at it." Julie got up and brushed off her backside. "You coming?"

"Of course."

They made their way across ancient junk and up the side of the pit where the tractor sat. Missy arrived first. Julie held back.

"Want me to look inside?"

Julie nodded.

Missy tiptoed up to the driver's side, stepped on the sidebar and peeked through the broken window. "Icky magazines. Gross. Like the ones by the mattress. There's a bunch of them sitting on the seat."

"Think its Brandon?"

"No. More like Kaleb." Missy remembered how Brandon held the door open for her at Dairy King, and how he acted like a gentleman.

"You're right," Julie agreed.

"You look in the passenger side."

Fear squeaked in Julie's voice, "What if it tips over?"

"Let me see. It's been sitting here in the pit for fifteen years. It looks like several people have been inside it. I don't think it'll move a centimeter with us on it."

"Whatever." Missy heard Julie's feet crunching on things as she made her way over.

Missy opened the dented door. It made a faint screech. "Can your door open up?"

Julie grunted and yelped when the metal on metal squealed. "What are we going to do?"

"You look for anything, under the seat, behind the seat."

Julie opened the passenger door and found a couple of candy wrappers. Missy reached under the front seat and grasped a pile of paper. She dragged them out and leafed through them. A small photograph fell face up. Missy nearly gasped; it was a picture of her mom. "Holy smoke."

"What is it?"

Missy held up the photograph.

Julie shook her head. "Hey, it's your school picture. Why's it here?" She turned it over and read the note on the back side.

Missy didn't feel good. She pushed the door all the way open, sat on the tractor's seat, and pointed to the picture. "It's not me. It's my mom. What's her picture doing in this tractor?"

"You two look alike."

She lifted the picture out of Julie's hand. "I can't stay here." Missy stepped off the tractor, put the picture in the jacket pocket, and headed quickly down the side of the pit to the bottom.

"This isn't heading home. You're going crazy on your not-making-sense thoughts. But glad you finally feel how I do."

"One more place to explore and I'm not going crazy."

"Go where?" Julie said as she tried to keep up with Missy.

"The shack."

Julie stopped. "Oh no, we aren't. It's haunted."

Missy stopped, turned and looked at Julie's face. "Daytime, nobody's there.

"Whatever. Fine. Why do I always do what you want to do?"

"At least I'm not like Maura or Ally."

"I'm not going to answer that comment," Julie smirked.

Missy ignored it and continued her walk up the side of the dirt pit to the shack.

"I'm scared."

"You're always scared. Take a deep breath and let it out slowly."

Julie rolled her eyes. "Like that's going to work."

"I just want to peek inside." Missy saw the backhoe parked and no car was in sight. "Only a second. I promise."

They reached the door, and with a slight hesitation, turned the nob and opened it. A small desk and chair were set on one side and a cot rested in an awkward place on the other side. It was almost like the person using it didn't want to sleep against the wall.

Julie looked at the walls and noticed the picture. "Look."

Missy studied it for a minute. "Oh, my heck. This is what was torn out of the paper at the library when Brandon and I were there." She looked at the bottom of the frame where the picture of her mom was inserted. "It's the same picture I found at the tractor." She took it out of her pocket and compared. "Jim. It's Jim, and he isn't dead. He's back to haunt his past?"

Sweat formed on Missy's forehead. She took off the jacket and tossed it on the cot.

"Let me see." Julie took the picture out of Missy's hand and put it aside the other. "Your life is getting stranger by the minute. No wonder you're starting to look like a ghost yourself."

"Gee, thanks for the compliment." *And I don't want to go back to the hospital and get a needle stuck in my arm.*

"Well, it's true. You hardly eat, look pale all the time, and now your face looks sick."

Missy touched her face and felt the heat. Her hands were cold as ice. She kept her head down and walked out the door. Julie followed and shut the door.

"I'm sorry, but you have me scared about you more than a ghost and bad dreams." She rubbed Missy's back as they walked home.

Tears formed in Missy's eyes. "I'm sorry. Maybe you're right. I'm going crazy. I almost feel like my parents are keeping a deep secret from me. Like they were involved in something bad along with Jim and he's come back for revenge. Something keeps me from finding out more about Jim, like there's a connection. It's making me mentally sick." She stopped at the end of the trail. "My parents took me to E.R during the night. I had bad nightmares that got out of hand. Mom thought I was having a seizure. So now I'm on sleeping pills so I can stay asleep. I didn't want to tell you. Now you know I have a problem."

Julie gave her a strong hug and Missy returned the gesture. "I don't think you're crazy and I hope the pills help you sleep and not have nightmares. I'm still worried."

"Thanks." Missy gave a half smile.

"Where's your jacket?" Julie asked.

Missy looked at herself. "Crap, I forgot it." She looked at the shack. "I'll get it later. It's not going anywhere."

Julie shrugged. "Call me later?"

"I will."

Julie headed home, looked back once and waved. Missy gave her a brave smile and wiped away her tears.

***

Missy's mom was in the kitchen when she walked in.

"Would you get me a big spoon, please?" She asked.

Missy took one from the drawer and handed it to her.

"Mom?"

"What, dear?"

Missy thought of the picture in her back pocket. "Um, forget it."

Mrs. Mack added milk and began to stir. "What is it?"

Missy didn't know what to do, but at last, took the picture out of her pocket, gave it to her mom, and waited. Her mom studied the picture, shaking her head. "This isn't your school picture."

"No. I believe it's you."

"You do look like me when I was your age. Where did you find it?" she handed it back and continued to stir the gravy.

"In the old tractor."

Mrs. Mack dropped the spoon on the floor. She turned around almost in slow motion, looked at Missy for a second, and smiled weakly.

"What were you doing in the pit? It's not safe, Missy. People throw junk in there and it's piled up. You shouldn't be hanging around in there. Were you alone?"

"No. Julie came with me. We were looking. Found a couple of magazines, candy wrappers, and your picture."

With a false laugh, Mrs. Mack said, "Kids can do the darnedest things, throwing trash and who knows what else anywhere they can. Remember, the pit is the junkyard for unreliable people. Someone must have cleaned out their storage and my picture happened to be in there. It's been years." She turned on the faucet and placed the spoon under the running water. "I'd better wash this off. Julia Child's five-second rule is long past." She turned away, but Missy could tell her mom was upset.

Missy headed back to her room not knowing what to think. Maybe Brandon was right in wanting to help her out. Out of bravery, she gave him a call.

"Brandon?"

"*Hi, Missy. What's going on?*" His voice sounded surprised she called.

"Want to do some snooping with me tonight?"

"Okay. In what?"

"I'll tell you tonight. Meet me at the end of my driveway at midnight. Bye." Missy's stomach twitched. She felt stupid for asking Brandon and worried about what he thought of her. Plan one was done and now for plan two.

She dialed again. "Julie, come spend the night tonight. I'll fill you in later." Missy called Ally and Maura and offered the same invitation.

Missy went to tell her parents and noticed the door was closed again. Feeling bad for a forming habit, she placed her ear to the door.

***

"Ray. Melissa found my picture in the old tractor at the pit. I heard her talk to Julie the other day on the phone about hearing backhoe noises at night. It has to be one of the reasons she's having nightmares."

"Have you called any of the counselors?"

"No. Some aren't listed on our insurance and I need to call them and ask."

"I think she needs some help soon. And honey, I'm sorry. Jim is dead. Why anyone is monkeying around there is a good question. There's nothing of value in the field unless the Forst family buried treasures or personal items in the coffins. People have complained but it seems nothing's been done or the authorities don't have enough evidence to do anything about it. And back to the pit, any one of your friends could have dropped your picture in the tractor a long time ago. If Missy says she found it there, it was protected from the rain. Jim's cousin supposedly ran the funeral home and now is dead with the grandparents. End of story."

"If the whole family is gone and the place is closed up, who could be using their backhoe on their field?"

Missy heard her dad give out an exasperated sigh. "As to why? I don't know. It doesn't mean anything."

"What would they be digging for? Some people say there are supposed to be people buried in the field. Could they be grave robbers looking for artifacts or jewelry?"

"I guess. It would be a matter for the sheriff. It's against the law to disturb graves," Mr. Mack said.

"Are you positive it doesn't have anything to do with what happened back then?"

Missy decided it was time to interrupt. "Mom?" She knocked on the bedroom door.

Mrs. Mack opened the door. "What, honey?" with a smile.

"I'm having a slumber party tonight. We're sleeping on the trampoline. Yes?"

"Fine with me. Glad you're feeling better though you still look a little pale."

"Thanks," Missy said.

"Do you think you need to take your prescription?" Mr. mack gestured toward the bathroom.

"I'll be fine with my friends. If I have a problem, I'll come and take one." *Tonight is the night and I need to stay awake to be at full alert.*

Chapter 30

Jim made a quick run back to the shack in the afternoon. He was past thinking he would get caught in the field during the daytime. He wasn't going to be seen, he'd be underground.

He wasn't sure what was needed until he did some research. He walked into the shack and went straight to the pictures on the wall. "Just looking at you from years ago makes my heart beat, Vi." He kissed it.

Jim turned to the corner, saw he covered the hole most of the way, and noticed a jacket on the cot. "Darn kids." He picked it up and saw it was a duplicate of his jacket. "Finders keepers."

He tossed it back on the cot, moved the lid over, and climbed down the ladder a few feet to the underground. Flashlight on, he saw damp spots on the ground which were set under the irrigation ditch. *Must have some metal in-between the dirt to hold the weight of the water.*

Jim saw three different tunnels. "Great, where should I start?" He pointed to the one on the left. "Eenie meenie mini mo, catch a tiger by the toe. If he hollers, let him

211

go." After three "Let him go," he went to the opening on the right. A few paces deeper in and he found it was a dead end. Solid dirt. The middle passage was the same. As he entered the third entrance, he felt his cell phone vibrate in his pocket.

The number was listed as private. *Probably Carlos. Not in the mood for another threat.*

"Hi, Jim. I got some customers at my business. They are waiting with smiles. Can you come?" Dwight sounded perky.

"I'll be there soon." Jim climbed up the ladder, excited for a drug sale, grabbed the jacket on the cot, and left.

***

Julie entered Missy's backyard from the gate and ambled over to the trampoline where Missy was doing flips.

Missy looked at her watch after doing her last back flip. "Maura and Ally should be here soon." She Jumped off the trampoline and headed towards the garage. "Want a pop? Got Sprite, Frosties's Root Beer, and Orange Crush."

"Orange Crush is good." Julie followed her inside. "I'll get some for our guests, too."

Maura and Ally came to the gate with their sleeping gear as Missy and Julie walked back to the trampoline. They dropped their belongings as Missy handed out the sodas.

"Now you're talking," Ally said. Maura nodded.

Maura and Julie took deep draws of their sodas.

"Tastes wonderful after dealing with the heat," Maura added.

"What's your plan?" Julie said.

Missy took a deep breath. "You're sleeping to cover for me." She took a big gulp of her root beer.

"Cover for you?" Maura asked.

"I'm meeting Brandon tonight and we're going to the cabin."

"What do you mean to the cabin?" Ally raised her eyebrows.

"To make a long story short, Julie and I went in it earlier today and found an old picture of my mom stuck on a corner of a picture frame. I don't want to get into full detail; Julie can fill you in when I'm gone."

Maura looked at Julie in question. "Am I going to be entertained?"

"Wait and see," Missy said.

"How did your mom's picture get in the shack?" Ally asked.

"I don't know, but Julie and I think this Jim dude who died years ago in the tractor race didn't. There was a cover up, and my parents know something they aren't telling me. I want to go back and see."

"Oh, my gosh. If they were involved in something, I'd know. How do you think your parents are involved?" Maura twiddled with her hair.

"What do you mean you'd know?"

"If my parents knew they would tell me." Maura took another drink.

Missy rolled her eyes. "Don't know, but it's the reason I'm going back to the shack to see if I can find anything else."

"What if he's there, or in the field digging?"

"That's another thing I'm trying to figure out. Why is he digging and why is it happening more often?"

"Aren't you afraid of being caught?" Ally grinned.

"Scared stiff, but with Brandon, I'll be safe."

"We hope so," Julie said and laid out her sleeping bag. The other girls got settled on the trampoline and watched an un-scary movie on Julie's laptop. Missy looked underneath the trampoline to reassure Julie there were no upside-down heads. The night passed quickly as they talked.

"What time is it?" Ally asked.

"Almost midnight," Missy said.

"Getting nervous?"

Missy sat up. "I think I can keep it together unless we meet the ghost-person or whatever."

"I'm glad you're brave. I doubt I'd go there even during the day," Ally said. She rolled onto her back and looked up. "A clear sky with lots of stars."

Julie shivered. "It better stay nice and clear for your sake. Remember our walk to the pit when we first met Brandon? The clouds came hovering in and made it dark and eerie."

"I remember more than I want to." Missy slipped her sneakers on. "Wait up for me."

"We will. And don't have too much fun," Maura said.

Not much of a chance, Missy thought. She slid through the gate, not closing it all the way.

Brandon waited on the side of the road. "Ready?" he asked.

"Way over ready, I want this over."

"Where do you want to go?" Brandon took Missy's hand as they walked. It was something Missy couldn't get enough of.

"To make a long story short, I found my mom's high school picture in the tractor at the dirt pit. Then we took our chances and went to the shack. Remember at the library the newspaper article about the tractor race torn out?"

"Yes."

"Well, it's nicely framed on the wall in the shack along with another high school picture of my mom. Either Jim is a ghost with lots of powers, or he never died. He came back to haunt."

Brandon squeezed Missy's hand. "But what if he's there now or in the field?"

"If we see a car, we'll run for our lives."

"And if he walks in on us, I've got my cell to bash him over the head and call 911."

"I feel safer." Missy grinned at Brandon.

They reached the door to the shack and noticed the backhoe set under the tree. There was no car in sight. Missy shivered. Brandon put his arm around her and turned the doorknob with his free hand. It opened with ease.

"Here goes," he took the first step inside.

"What if he's waiting for us?"

With his cell phone flashlight app on, Brandon panned the light around the small shack and saw nothing. Missy's jacket was no longer on the cot.

"It's gone."

"What's gone?"

"I forgot to include in my explanation I had left my mom's jacket here earlier." She looked under the cot. Missy plugged her nose. "It smells like dirty socks." She turned to the picture frame. "Look. Here's the article and my mom's picture."

Brandon held up his cell for more light. "You look the same except the eye color." He put his hand under Missy's chin to lift her face.

Missy wasn't sure if he would kiss her or was comparing eye color. She held her breath.

Brandon motioned to the cot and looked behind it in the corner. "This is interesting."

"What?"

"There is a hole. Looks like a basement of some sort under the shack.

"How could that be? In the dirt? And I thought it couldn't get more bizarre than it is." Missy tiptoed to the small desk to see. "Here's something else."

Brandon slid the desk out from the wall. "Empty gas tank. I bet it's for the backhoe.

"I'll be darned."

He flashed the beam around the shack again. A small screech pierced the air. Brandon whacked his head on the corner of the picture frame and it fell to the ground. "Ow!"

Missy touched his head gently as she examined it. "Is it bleeding?"

He grimaced and turned his head as Missy touched where the frame hit. "No." He aimed the flashlight at the floor. "Stupid picture frame." He picked it up and hung it back on the wall.

Missy made sure her mom's picture was in place.

"Screech. Scritch."

"Hear it?" Missy grabbed Brandon's arm and got herself closer.

They turned to face the door and a faint light beamed through the thick glass window.

Again, another *"Shriek"*.

Brandon turned his phone light off and touched a finger to his lips.

Chapter 31

Jim arrived back to the shack to do some more digging. After he parked his car, he saw a light flickering in the shack and shadows through the window.

For a minute, he had worried Carlos followed him from New Mexico to pay him a surprise visit. But more likely it was teenagers coming to a private place to party.

There wasn't anything important inside; *did I put the piece of wood back over the hole in the corner? I don't remember if I did.* Jim rubbed his forehead and knew he had to get whoever was in out and crossed his fingers they wouldn't see the hole to the tunnels. He had put the cot over it out of common sense.

He decided to scare them off for good. He picked up a few small rocks, sneaked to the back of the shack, and stood by the small window. He heard faint talking. The thought of giving them a good scare made him smile. He flicked one of the small rocks against the window.

Crack!

***

Brandon and Missy looked towards the window.

"I didn't hear a car pull up."

"Preoccupied. Let's go," Brandon said as they hurried out the door fast as they could.

They sprinted past the rope tree. Missy stopped hard. "Something's got my neck!" she cried out.

Brandon turned around and ran back to her.

He reached behind her, felt a branch tangled in the back of her shirt, and twisted it off. "It's a branch. Seems like this path has a curse on you."

"What do you mean?" Missy rubbed her neck and felt like an idiot.

"Every time you're on it, you trip, fall, or run into something."

Missy shivered. She didn't like the sound of the curse, but she didn't want to show Brandon how much it scared her.

"That didn't come out right," he said sheepishly.

"You're right, it didn't." She dropped her hand away from his and folded her arms. She wasn't going to admit he had touched a nerve. She turned away and began walking toward her house.

"Can I say I'm sorry? I am." Brandon jogged to catch up.

She looked across the field at the shack.

"A little scary for me, too." He ran his hand through her hair and she turned around.

Before Missy could answer, Brandon's lips were on hers. Missy's stomach tightened up in knots in a feel-good way. Her face tingled. It seemed to last forever. He

219

stopped and gave a soft smile. "Good enough for a sorry?"

"I think so."

"Only think?"

"Yes." They walked back to the front of Missy's house in silence. *I don't know what to say after his kiss. Does Brandon feel it was a mistake?*

Missy was glad her mom wasn't up with the light on. *What if my friends got loud laughing and my mom checked up on them and noticed I wasn't there? I'm walking on the edge but can't help it. I have to find out about Jim.*

"Goodnight. I'll call you soon." Brandon walked away, turned and waved, then disappeared into the darkness.

Missy put her fingertips to her lips. She relived the kiss in her mind to make sure it had happened. She was a little dizzy when she got back to the trampoline. Her friends were still up and waiting.

"Did my mom poke her head out the door?"

"No, but Tommy peeked out once and said he was making sure we were okay. He couldn't tell you were gone." Ally said.

"That's a relief."

Maura sat up. "You've been gone a long time."

Missy crawled into her sleeping bag. "It was creepy, and I didn't get mom's jacket back. She will not be happy."

"You're shaking," Ally said.

"There was something else."

Maura drew closer. "Tell us," Ally and Julie crowded around.

"Brandon kissed me," she squealed.

"Are you serious? I'm sooo jealous." Julie grinned. "How did it happen?"

"Do you need to have the birds and the bees explained, Julie?" Maura asked. "You put your lips on his lips."

"I know. But tell us. Was it a nice long kiss?"

Missy grinned. "At least five seconds. It felt like forever."

"Was it good?" Ally asked.

Smiling, Missy lay, still grinning. "Best five seconds ever. But I'm getting tired. It's been one heck of a night."

"Your mom's jacket? What're you going to do?" Julie looked worried.

"I don't know. I'm going to have to figure it out. Tomorrow."

"Someone took it?" Maura said.

"Looks like it."

"But who?" Ally asked.

Maura gave Ally a look. "The guy in the shack, of course. He's not a ghost."

"Maura's right. But now I have to get to sleep." Missy said.

She snickered. "Hello, dreamland."

Missy was still grinning as she drifted off to sleep.

Chapter 32

Jim got up early Saturday morning and went back to the shack with paper and pen in hand. He'd gotten a hardhat with an attached headlight and was set to discover his masterpiece treasure. Every day he was feeling more and more pressure from his lack of progress.

He hoped everything he needed was there, his life was at stake and knew sooner or later Carlos, or any gang member of Rock's Edge, would track him down for good. The threatening calls were coming multiple times daily. Jim ignored the calls and hoped they thought he was busy making Twist.

The third tunnel after a few feet led to a storage area, more like the size of a den, with another opening to the left large enough to fit about eight coffins. Only three were there, filled with counterfeit money, several bags of Twist, and the notebook on how to make Twist. Jim was ecstatic. "Hallelujah. I can't believe I found it. I'm free, I'm alive!" He'd hit the mother lode, finally.

Jim picked up some dirt and threw it like confetti. It wasn't all dirt. Some type of hard objects landed on his hardhat and bounced to the ground. *"What was that?"* He aimed his light down and saw two arrowheads. *Interesting.*

***

Tommy ran out of the house and tried to find a place to jump on the trampoline without landing on one of the four girls.

"Wake up wake up. Mommy has pancakes!"

"Ugh. Not again, Tommy. We're sleeping," Missy groaned.

"Got to hurry. Mom and Dad are leaving."

"Guess it means we have to leave, too," Maura mumbled. She got up and rolled her sleeping bag. Ally copied, and Julie still lay dazed in hers.

"Don't forget the pancakes," Tommy said as he ran back inside the house.

"I'll forget the pancakes, go home and sleep more comfortable on my bed," Maura said. "Thanks for the interesting night."

Missy wasn't sure if her comment was sarcastic or true.

Ally stood with her belongings. "It was an interesting night on your part," and pointed to Missy. "See you later." She followed Maura in silence.

Julie got up and gathered her belongings. "I'm not hungry. I got stuffed with your excitement last night. So happy for you Missy, and I'll call you later." She hugged Missy and left.

Missy dragged herself inside and was greeted by her mom, "Where are your friends? I have plenty of pancakes."

"To tired to be hungry." Missy sat at the counter and laid her head in her arms.

"You can get a twenty-minute power nap. Dad and I need to go to Boise, so you and Tommy can do something to stay busy."

"Fine." Missy retrieved her bedding from the trampoline and curled up on her bed. She could hear Tommy watching cartoons downstairs. She was drifting off to sleep again when the phone rang.

Gosh darn stupid phone. "Hello," she grumbled.

"You don't sound happy," Julie said.

"I'm trying to get a cat nap. You should be sound asleep too. You barely left my house." Missy yawned and rolled over.

"I'm awake now after walking home. I got excited thinking about your kiss last night."

Missy didn't answer for a moment. "I can't believe it happened. Me. Brandon kissed me."

"I know, right? I could tell Maura was disturbed about it. I think she's doing her best to have Brandon like Ally."

"He has all the chances he has being at Kaleb's all the time. Maybe he's trying to make her jealous by liking me?"

"No way, Jose. He likes you. You stuck watching Tommy today?"

"Whatever. Want to come over again?"

"Can't. My parents want me to go with them to pick out new horse gear. Not sure where we're going."

Missy thought about getting out of bed. She made it as far as sitting. Good enough.

"Hold on for a sec," Julie replied.

Missy heard the sound of stomping feet through the house. She sat for a long moment waiting when Tommy galloped into her room.

"I'm bored, Missy."

She pointed to the phone.

He hopped up on the bed beside her. "I want a ride on the Dirt bike." He bounced on the mattress.

"Not now, phone. See?"

"Please. I want to dig for arrowheads." He smiled.

"No." She held up her hand to stop him.

"I'm back," Julie said.

"What took you so long? The Tidy Bowl Man got you in the toilet?"

"Ha ha. No. I had to see where my parents were. Don't want them busting in."

"Missy," Tommy said. He patted her leg to get her attention. "Missy, I want to dig."

"Not now." She pushed his hand off. "Go dig in your sandbox." Tommy gave her the evil look of death and marched out. Within seconds she heard the back door slam shut.

"What did he want?" Julie asked.

"Wanted me to take him for a ride to the field. He wants to dig for arrowheads."

"Sounds like fun ... or not."

"Not."

"Ya. Sounds like my parents are ready to go. Talk to you later."

"K. Have fun and bye."

Missy got up and went to the bathroom. She still heard the television, but the show wasn't what Tommy would watch, so she knew he was still outside in the back yard. She brushed her teeth, turned off the T.V., and went out the back door. She didn't see her little brother.

"Tommy? Where are you?"

No answer.

She scouted around the backyard and looked in the sandbox thinking he buried himself and was dead from choking on sand. No sign, but fresh footsteps. And his plastic shovel and bucket weren't there. *Dang, where did he go?* She hustled back inside, ran to the front door and called his name.

Nothing.

Her stomach knotted and she felt like puking. If anything happened to her little brother, she'd be dead meat. She searched his room and the basement. "Tommy, where are you? Stop hiding from me." She ran upstairs. "I'll take you for a ride."

No answer. This wasn't looking good. Missy was in deep doo-doo. The big sister was not allowed to lose the little brother. She ran out the back door and didn't bother to shut it. Leaping on her dirt bike, she cruised down the road and around the neighborhood. No sign of him. She drove to the tree ditch, parked, and looked around in the field. She didn't see Tommy, but his bucket and shovel sat a few feet further in. *Crap! He has to be somewhere around here.*

Missy was irked and needed to have a little talk with him for taking unsupervised excursions like this. But first, she had to find him. Where did he go? She wasn't sure if she should yell or keep looking?

***

Jim had sniffed so much Twist, he needed to find a way to calm down and think straight. Fresh air would help. He climbed up the ladder and put his hard hat on the small table when he heard a knock on the door.

Ha, if it's Carlos or anyone else, I'm safe. He opened the door and stepped back when he saw the face of a little boy.

***

Missy hated to think Tommy walked to the shack and if so, went inside. Who knew what could happen? Around the little curved path, she saw Tommy standing in the shack doorway. The butterflies in Missy's stomach had worked their way up to her throat, and she had a hard time swallowing. She stopped to listen. Someone was talking, then she heard Tommy say, "Thank you."

Missy was sweating when she edged up behind Tommy. Looking into the shack, and standing four feet in front of her, was the man she had seen at the parade. Their eyes latched.

"Looks like we have a visitor," Jim said.

Tommy turned around. "Missy, see what I got?" He tried to show her what was in his hand, but she shook her head still gazing at Jim.

"Not now. I think we should go." Missy placed both hands on his shoulders and broke the staring spell. "Sorry

227

for my brother bothering you." She turned Tommy around and pushed him away from the door.

"No problem," the man called out. "He didn't bite."

When they got to Missy's dirt bike, she turned and put her face a few inches from his. "How dare you leave without telling me? How could you?"

"I... you... but..." a tear wended down his face. "He's a nice man. I think he knows Mom and Dad."

Whoa. "What do you mean?"

"I told him who our parents were, and he smiled."

Missy kicked the kickstand up, climbed on, grabbed Tommy, and hauled him on board. She looked at him again, more sternly. "You know you're not supposed to talk to strangers?"

"Yesss, but this is different."

"No, it's not. You will not talk to strangers. Do you hear me?"

He nodded.

"And now we're going home, hold on."

Missy felt his small arms reach around her waist and knew he was crying. She wasn't in the mood to talk. She throttled the engine and drove home faster than she ever had before. Missy wanted to get away from the shack. She wheeled the bike into the garage, parked it in her usual spot, and hurried inside. Tommy was back in front of the T.V. set and Missy was in her bedroom reading. Her parents drove into the driveway forty-five minutes later.

***

Jim watched as Missy dragged Tommy away as she could. If he hadn't sniffed some Twist, he would have been a nervous wreck. If he showed any signs of frustration, he knew Missy would pick it up. He hoped they didn't see the hole in the floor, even though Jim stood right by it.

He remembered the jacket left the other night. Violet's jacket. It still smelled like she did many years ago. He forgot what perfume she wore, but it didn't matter. He snuggled the jacket at night and dreamed of Violet.

The kid had some of his mom's look, but more like Ray. Violet's daughter was almost a look-alike for her mom as a teenager. Violet. Jim sighed, found his car keys, and drove to the funeral home to mellow out.

Chapter 33

"You spent this whole morning reading?" Mrs. Mack peeked halfway into Missy's room.

"Not the whole time." Missy placed the book on her nightstand and sat from her nice comfortable position. "Did you have fun?"

"Business meetings are always fun." She gave a wry smile. "We wives do our best not to yawn while the men talk business."

"Fun, fun."

Missy's mom didn't answer and rested against the door frame. "Looks like your dad will be traveling shortly, too."

"Oh." Missy supposed she could have shown a little extra interest, but she'd had enough excitement. Besides, it was still morning and she was getting hungry.

Mom took the hint and changed the subject. "Speaking of food, guess who we ran into at the grocery store?"

"Santa Claus?"

Mrs. Mack came into the room. "Funny," and patted Missy's head. "We saw Brandon and his parents."

"Nice."

"They invited us over for dinner tonight."

Missy felt her face get warm. "Dinner?" Her stomach churned.

"Your cheeks look a little red. We can call and cancel." Mrs. Mack knew Missy blushed, but liked to play with her at times.

"Oh, no. Dinner sounds fine."

"I thought so." She left the room chuckling.

Why did Brandon's parents want my family to come for dinner? I can't wait to see what's going on.

***

They arrived at the Miller's at 6:30 p.m. Missy managed to get a few hours' sleep in the afternoon. She didn't want to be yawning her way through the meal.

"Hello Melissa, Mr. and Mrs. Mack." Mrs. Miller greeted them at the front door. "Come in."

"Call me Violet, and this is Ray." Missy's mom noticed the shoes against the wall and placed hers beside them.

"And I'm Rita. So nice to meet you."

"You must be Dean?" Mr. Mack extended his hand.

"Come in and have a seat. Dinner will be ready soon." Missy's and Brandon's dads walked to the living room and watched the sports section of the news. They liked some of the same teams and were talking about the baseball season.

"Do you need last minute help in the kitchen, Rita?" Mrs. Mack asked.

"No, we are set. Take a seat. I'm bringing it out." Mr. Miller saw his wife head back to the kitchen and went in to help.

At the table, Brandon sat across from Missy as his mom sat to his right side. Tommy sat by Missy, with Mrs. Mack on the other side of her. Mr. Miller and Mrs. Mack sat at each end of the table.

Brandon's mom, being super smooth, stepped up. "I heard you were in track." She smiled at Missy. "Brandon does track but missed out this year with the move. What races did you do?"

Missy smiled. "Hurdles, and the 200 and 400 relays."

Mr. Miller put down his fork. "How can you jump over those hurdles?"

"Limber," Brandon said. "Missy is a gymnast, too I heard. She's flexible."

"I did some gymnastics in my high school years. I enjoyed it," Mrs. Miller said. "What's your favorite? Mine was Beam."

"Wow. I'm impressed. The beam is my worse because gravity is my enemy." Everyone chuckled. "My favorite is the floor."

"I enjoy watching gymnastics competitions, and what they do now is a lot more difficult than I ever had to do. I wish you well." Brandon's mom said.

"Thank you." Missy could feel the red heat on her face.

Dinner went on pleasantly with casual talk when Mr. Miller, noticed Tommy kept putting his hand in his front pocket. "What do you like to do during the summer?"

"I go digging."

"What do you dig for?" He could tell Tommy had a pocket full of treasures.

"Arrowheads."

"Fun. Have you found any?"

Tommy nodded. "Wanna see? A nice man gave this to me." He pulled his hand out of his pocket. "I dug this one up at a grave place for Native Americans. I got another one in the field."

"Field?" Brandon's dad looked puzzled.

"Un-hunh. Across the street by the tree ditch."

"How many arrowheads do you have now?"

Missy was getting a little edgy. She didn't know where the questions were leading. When Tommy took out the second arrowhead, she kneed his leg to signal him. He ignored her.

"This is two." He put them on the table and reached back into his pocket, "I got this one today and now I have three." He grinned to everyone at the table.

Missy's mom looked him in the eye. "Where did you get it?"

Missy kneed Tommy again. He squinted his face.

"By the field, too, you say?" Missy's dad asked.

"No, it's the one the man gave me." Tommy turned to his dad. "Will we be cursed?"

"Cursed? Why?" Mrs. Mack asked Tommy. She turned to Missy and said in a different voice, "You never told me Tommy left this morning."

Tommy wasn't listening, he was simply happy to be getting attention. "The man told me if you give something away and tell on them, you'll be cursed, or maybe the Native American will be cursed. I forget."

Mom and Dad both looked at Missy. "We'll talk about this later," her dad said.

Missy knew she was busted. Tommy didn't think it was something to talk about later. "Missy said she was sleeping but was on the phone instead." He kept looking at his arrowheads.

Missy had to cover herself. "When Tommy decided to walk across the street and dig in the field. When I woke up, um, got off the phone, I figured out where Tommy had gone. I drove over there and he was talking to a guy at the shack. He seemed nice, but we didn't stay long. I grabbed Tommy and left. I guess he gave Tommy the arrowhead."

Brandon kept his lips closed the whole time. Brandon's dad looked at both Brandon and Melissa. "It would be better if everyone stayed away from the shack. Better yet, don't go over to the tree or the pit." He sat back in his chair. "For your own safety."

"Mind if I ask what's going on?" Mr. Mack asked.

Mrs. Mack listened as the conversation became more detailed. She looked at Mrs. Miller. "Would you mind if I show Tommy where the T.V. is and let him watch a movie or play some games?" Mrs. Miller nodded.

Mr. Miller and Mr. Mack noticed to keep quiet. Tommy's eyes lit. "I can play a game? I don't know how."

"You can choose a movie, and I do believe there are some army toys in the room, too. Come on, I'll show you." Mr. Miller led Tommy to a room down the hall.

Missy looked at Brandon, then down at the table. She wasn't sure what would happen, but had the feeling she was in serious trouble. Brandon's mom came back and took her seat.

Brandon's dad got right to the point. "I have a bit of information to pass along and it's serious. I can't and shouldn't say a word, but I'll fill you in this much." He tapped his fingers on the table before speaking again. "I don't want our kids or anyone's kids hanging around the field or in the pit. Enough said."

Both mothers glanced at each other again. "You wouldn't know this if it's what I think you aren't saying, but we did have problems here in Nampa when Violet and I were in high school. There was a fuss about drugs and gangs. The way we understood it, the police had taken care of it." Mr. Mack said.

"I can only reiterate that the shack, the pit, and the whole area are now off-limits," Mr. Miller reiterated. "Understand?" Brandon was sitting still; Missy nodded and knew they were going to break the rules.

Chapter 34

Not far from the funeral home on Main Street was the Country Pantry Café. After a long afternoon nap, nothing sounded better than a home-cooked meal. Jim walked a few blocks to the Pantry and sat in a corner booth, mulling his thoughts.

He still couldn't believe he'd finally found the lot. Good ol' Dwight was like a puppet ready to do whatever Jim wanted. He knew Dwight had dollar signs in his eyes and would help him clean out the tunnel.

"Here you go, sir. Let me know if you need anything else." The waitress set the plate loaded with a medium rare steak, baked potato with green beans, and a roll in front of Jim. She set a glass of wine on the rocks next to his plate. The aroma steamed off the steak as he took his first bite.

The café door opened; the jingling bell snapped Jim out of his thoughts. He looked up and saw Ruth. She smiled.

For a redhead, she was a babe. Might have to celebrate with her tonight.

She gave her order and sidled over to Jim's table.

"Mind if I join you?"

He wouldn't have been surprised if she had said, "*Hiya, cowboy.*"

"Have a seat." He pointed to the bench across the table from him.

"I just got off work and I don't feel like cooking."

"I know how you feel," he replied. "No dinner with your dad tonight?".

"My dad?"

"Dwight?"

"Yes. I figured you find out." She raised her eyebrows. "My dad keeps to himself and doesn't interfere with my personal life."

Maybe having the connection between father and daughter will be for the better. Busy in the day with Dwight, relaxing at night with Ruth. Jim looked up to see the waitress approaching. "Looks like you have a salad on its way."

The waitress placed the plate in front of Ruth along with a bottle of Ranch dressing.

Jim had to admit to himself, he liked how easy she was to talk to. They laughed and even touched hands across the table. Things were looking good until the café door jingled for new customers coming inside.

"But, Mom, it didn't happen that way," A teenage girl was in the midst of an explanation.

"You two can talk after we order," The girl's father said.

"Never mind. I don't want to talk about it," the teenager grumped. "You two wouldn't understand."

237

"Try us, Julie. We might," The mother said.

Jim watched the waitress take the family's order carefully. His fork had stopped halfway to his mouth.

Ruth tapped Jim's hand. "Hey. Where'd you go?"

Jim stared at the girl's mother. *I know that face. It's Violet's friend from High School, Rachel. They were more together than I was with Violet.*

Mr. Miller ordered as the family took a seat at the booth behind Ruth. The adults sat facing Jim.

Julie's mom leaned across the table and whispered a conversation with her. The conversation was interrupted when the waitress arrived at their table with appetizers.

Not good. Rachel still lives here and probably still is Violet's close friend. It is time to go. He couldn't take a chance for her to recognize him.

Ruth tapped Jim's arm again and he looked back at her. "Do you know them?"

"Them? No. I was thinking of work, getting the funeral home taken care of." He took another bite of his steak. "It's taking a little longer, with the paperwork, taxes, and legal stuff. You know how it is."

Julie stayed quiet as her parents started a conversation about horses. Jim was trying to think of how to get out of the restaurant when Rachel looked over at Jim and froze, nearly choking on her water.

"Mom, are you okay?"

"Y-yess." She cleared her throat. "Water went down the wrong pipe." Her husband rubbed her back.

"Ruth." Jim gave a soft smile and got a bogus fifty-dollar bill out of his wallet.

She looked back at him with hope. "Yes?"

With his eyes, he indicated the door and pushed his plate to the middle of the table. "I'm done." He took her hand, placed the money on the table, and led Ruth out the door without looking back. He could see by Ruth's face she was going to be happy.

Chapter 35

Violet swallowed another drink of her Diet Pepsi, calming her nerves after the interesting evening at the Miller's. The phone light lit and she answered it on the second ring.

"Hi, Violet. It's Rachel."

"How are you?"

"Same ol' same ol'."

"What's up?"

"Listen, I know it's a little late to be calling. We took Julie out for a Country Pantry dinner. Can we meet for a few minutes? Let's say in your back field in five minutes?"

She paused, sensing concern in her friend's, Rachel Brown's, who was Julie's mom's, voice. "Of course. I'll be right out."

Both women had been lucky enough to purchase their childhood homes. Their special meeting place had always been by the ancient apple tree nestled in Mack's back field, only two houses away from the Brown's house.

A huge limb, bending nearly to the ground before branching skyward again, created a convenient place to sit and talk privately.

"Something on your mind?" Violet leaned against the low limb.

Rachel pulled a few long grass strands and braided them. Her hands shook in the process. "I'm curious. Did Jim Forst have any siblings?"

She expressed a look of shock. It was a question out of nowhere. "He was an only child. There might be a cousin or two in there somewhere besides Nate who died recently. Why?"

Rachel pulled out another strand of grass. "Because I could have sworn, I saw Jim tonight. Either it was him, his double, or a cousin. I have a look-alike cousin. At family gatherings, we've been mistaken for each other, I know it happens."

"You don't believe in ghosts?"

"True. Heck, it could have been a complete stranger who looks like Jim. Whoever it was, I saw him with the woman who works at the antique store."

She shrugged. "Honey, Jim's dead, and since neither of us believes in ghosts, there's a good-looking guy, who looks a bit like Jim. Same height, same look, same build, a few strands of gray hair, and a couple of wrinkles. It's been fifteen years." Violet crossed her arms and shivered at a sudden cold breeze.

She remembered the grocery store encounter. "I think I know who you mean. Got a glimpse of a guy not too long ago at the store who looked like Jim, but I know it's not. It can't be. I even talked to Ray about it. All of us saw him get rolled over." *But no one else could have those shiny blue eyes.* "Did you know noses and ears still grow in your adulthood? It's not him, because Jim is dead, God rest his soul. It's funny. Me telling you this. I was the one with the broken heart." Violet grew quiet for a moment.

"But we never saw the casket open, did we?"

"No. Shut and sealed. His parents didn't want to upset us. When the EMTs pulled him out from under the tractor, he was in a messed up state." She stood and brushed the dirt and loose bark off her back side. "Can I tell you something?"

Rachel nodded.

"Tommy took off across the street during the day without Missy's knowledge and talked to a gentleman at the shack. We had dinner with the Millers tonight and shared it with Brandon's dad, Dean. He's a DEA and told us to keep our kids away from the pit and the shack."

Violet shivered again. "I've been hearing backhoe noises at night, so I wonder if it's the police digging for something, or the shack guy is digging and the police haven't caught him yet. It's kept Missy awake and upsetting her. We ended up taking her to ER for some sleeping pills."

"I'm sorry."

"Has Julie said anything to you? I'm sure if she was worried, she'd tell you, so you could tell me."

"Julie has said nothing about it to me. But they are teenagers, and parents don't understand a thing."

"True." She remembered.

Rachel touched her dear friend's hand and gave it a soft squeeze. "I have a question. You don't have to answer it."

"You want to know if I might still love Jim, don't you?"

She glanced at her as if shy. "I suppose. He was the most interesting guy in high school. He looked like a combination of *Kevin Bacon* and *Anthony McCarthy glued together* with blonde hair, and sea blue eyes. We all had the hots for him, but you were the one he liked."

"I know. It took me a while to understand me as his girlfriend was not a good idea. I had to make a choice. It was him or Ray. I'm glad I choose Ray. Can you imagine Jim being responsible for children?"

She chuckled. "No, and I'm sorry to dump this on you."

"You're not dumping anything. I'm glad you called. Thanks, Rachie."

She snickered. "High school nickname."

Violet. "It came back. It seemed natural. We had fun."

"We did and I'd like to do this again."

"For a better reason, though."

"I'll talk to you soon, Vi."

Smiling, she nodded and headed back to the house.

Chapter 36

Bright sunshine warmed Missy's skin as she floated in the pool trying to catch up on a sleepless night. Coming home from Brandon's house the night before, stressed her out. She wanted to tell her mom she knew Jim was alive, but didn't want to add more trouble for snooping around.

Julie had mentioned several times she was worried about Missy and her change of attitude. *Am I going bonkers?*

"Missy, you have a visitor," Her mom called from the back door.

Missy sat on her mattress and paddled over to the edge of the pool. Brandon peeped out and offered a weak smile.

"Did you bring your trunks? A wonderful day for a swim and a tan."

He smiled. "Are you trying to tell me something?"

She laughed. "Of course not. A little tan never hurt. It proves you didn't sit inside all summer."

He kicked off his sandals, sat on the deck and put his feet into the water beside her.

"What brought you here? Bored and decided to come and be bored with me?"

Brandon stirred the water with his feet. "I need your help. We need to go back to the shack again."

"We were told by your dad last night to never step foot in there for a very, very long time."

"I know, but it's bugging me. I want to see what's in the hole and how deep it goes."

"Do you think we'll find anything?"

Brandon splashed water on her and grinned. "I've learned a thing or two from my dad."

"And how to disobey him." Missy smiled. A cold shiver went up her spine. "What if a ghost or Jim catches us?"

"I'm not afraid. Are you?" He ran his hand through his hair. "So."

Missy paddled closer and touched his foot. It sent more tingles through her body. "What time?" His eyes widened for a split second. Missy caught electricity in his eyes and smiled.

Brandon looked at his cell, "It's 10:00 am. I'll be by around 1:00 pm." He stood. "K?"

She nodded. Missy had acted brave and cool, but it felt conspiratorial and a little dangerous. At least she would find out what was going on, and she wouldn't be alone. Brandon's hadn't visited on a tease.

"By the way, you're getting tan. Looks good." He waved and left through the back gate before he could see her blush. She could feel the heat like the sun on her face and smiled. Things were getting better and better.

The gate closed and Missy's mom came back out. "What did Brandon say? It sounded important."

Missy made whirls in the water with her hands. "He wants to go for a walk around the neighborhood later. I said yes."

"Were you going to ask me first before you said yes?"

Missy shrugged "You know he's nice and his parents are nice, too. I figured you wouldn't mind." She gave the most innocent face ever.

"Around the neighborhood? You're not thinking of snooping across the street are you, it's legally off limits. You heard Mr. Miller."

"No. I'll show him where I ride my motorcycle in the ditch behind his house and other areas. Nothing to worry about."

"I don't want you out late, no matter how nice he is."

"Yes, Mom." And saw her scanning her body.

"Get out of the water."

Missy did with no argument.

She waited. "Turn around," she ordered and moved her finger in a circle.

Missy turned.

"You're cooked. Time to cover up before you turn into leather."

"At least no one can say I spent the summer indoors." Missy slid into a t-shirt. "Can I go back in if I leave the shirt on? I'd like to do a few more laps."

"Five minutes."

She slipped into the water and swam two laps as her mom watched, then went back into the house. Around the fourth or fifth lap, the back fence gate opened and Julie walked in.

"Hi, Missy."

"Hi, hop on in?"

"It's why I'm here." Julie looked over at the back door making sure Missy's mom wasn't peering out and lowered her voice. "I wanted to see if you figured anything else." Julie moved closer. "You know, the tractor ghost?"

Missy splashed water on her legs.

"Hey, watch it."

"Got some information, and are you coming in or not?" Missy back-stroked away. "Major news flash: Brandon was here and wants to go for a long walk."

"Nice," Julie slipped out of her shirt and shorts revealing a swimsuit underneath. She leaped in like a cannon ball causing a huge spray.

"Good one."

"I came over to ask if you heard about last night," Julie rowed over on the other mattress she jumped on after her cannon ball.

"I know mom went to talk to your mom but she didn't tell me anything. Brandon's dad told us to stay away from the pit and the shack. Off limits, or else."

"Your mom told my mom, and she told me what happened last night at Brandon's house. She wanted to make sure you and I weren't going to dangerous places we shouldn't be going to."

"Our parents know we go to the pit and the tree ditch. Where else can we go?"

"I don't know, but we went out to eat last night and my mom nearly choked when she was drinking her water. She was looking at a guy sitting across from her. The guy and his date left shortly after. My mom was silent the rest of the evening." Julie kicked her feet gently in the water.

"And when we got home and she talked to your mom, she told me more about who Jim was, and how serious he and your mom were. It's almost like they would have gotten married if your dad didn't move here and catch her eye. I like your, dad." Julie smiled at Missy.

Missy floated around in circles making small waves with the mattress. "My life, including my parents, is confusing. No wonder I need to figure out why Jim's back and not dead. There is a secret and I want to find out what it is. I know it involves me. Were my parents dealing drugs in High School and got caught or almost did? Was Jim the dealer and pushed my parents around to sell drugs? I've got to find out."

"I'm sure something will settle soon, if and when they catch Jim or the ghost of Jim."

"I hope so." Missy rolled off her mattress.

An hour passed with laps, routines, and chit-chat about nothing. Missy swam to the pool's edge. "Whew, I think I'm done for the day and need to rest before my walk with Brandon."

"You must have been in a long time before I came. Our shortest time in the pool is three hours."

"I was. I like to think of it as a runaway vacation. People like Maura and Ally would be on their computers or cells. Heck, I'm sure Maura's on her cell when she's riding her horse. I, with no privileges, get to live the simple life." They sat on the side of the pool with their legs dangling in the water drying off.

"Um, do you think that's all I do, too?"

"I know you chat on your cell and do whatever you like to do on your laptop, but you got a horse and take care of him. You come over here to see me. If I had a cell, you'd text me and our relationship would be best-text-only friends." Missy knew she jabbered nonsense words but didn't want Julie to worry. "You see there's more to life than all the other crap."

Julie wrapped her towel around her shoulders. "I get what you're saying. Heck, my parents didn't get me my cell until I was 14. I'm still not sure why I need it, but they figured if anything happened when I was on my horse, I could make the call." Julie got up, wrapped the towel around her waist and grabbed her clothes.

"Oh, I forgot to ask. Where are you walking?"

"The long way around the block." And winked.

"What are you getting into Missy? How out of the way is the walk?"

"We found a hole in the corner of the shack the night I went to find my mom's jacket. I also didn't tell you Jim almost caught us inside. He parked by the shed and didn't hear the car."

"Are you serious? Why didn't you tell me?"

"Well, for one thing, my mind was erased from everything after the kiss," Missy smiled.

"Makes sense." Julie smiled back.

"So, Brandon wants to see what's under the shack. Might see a ghost or hidden treasures."

Julie nodded. "Your parents won't like it."

"They'll never find out."

"Keep me posted," Julie said. "I'll call you tomorrow. I want to hear the full details." She winked and the gate banged shut as she left.

Chapter 37

Jim got comfy on his couch and felt on top of the world. He enjoyed his night with Ruth and got a few hours of sleep. Even when he got the phone call from Carlos, he was past feeling nervous.

"It's all there, dude. Every single bit. My grandparents were busy with Nate for the past several years. Who knew why they didn't tell my parents or me," Jim took another sniff of Twist. "Me and my buddy will be packing up and hitting the road tonight or in the early morning."

"How much are you taking?"

"Enough to last us for a few weeks. I don't want to make a scene with a car jammed to the top with boxes."

"I want my share doubled. No more waiting, and to make sure, I'm on my way." Carlos hung up.

On his way? If he finds my hiding place, he'll take full control. He'll want to take it all and control my usage. Carlos will dig me back in a hole for good. Jim sat up and decided to drive out to Dwight's work instead of calling him and telling him the good and bad news.

251

Dwight walked around his storage shed when Jim pulled in. It looked like Dwight was trying to stay busy. Jim got out of his car. "How fast can you close and come with me?"

Dwight jogged over. "As fast as you want me to. Why?"

Jim couldn't help but give a big smile. "We are rich. I got my stuff but need to hurry and get it out of town. You in?"

Dwight looked at Jim, back at his car lot, and back to Jim. "Give me five minutes." He ran into his office, then emerged with his briefcase and got in Jim's car. "I grabbed a couple more dealers' plates in case we need them on the way."

Jim didn't reply but thought, *it's a good idea, but will Dwight be traveling with me to Arizona? Will he take what I give him in payment? I'll play it by ear.*

***

Brandon arrived at 1:00 pm. "Ready?" he took a step into the foyer. "Hi, Mrs. Mack." She had come around the corner from the kitchen.

"Hi, Brandon. So, tell me. You're going for a walk around the block and Missy's going to show you where she rides her motorcycle, correct?" She looked at Missy. "Why don't you give him a ride?"

Oh boy, I didn't think of that one. "Cross country will start in a few weeks before school and we want to start getting in shape. Plus, I like walking?" Missy didn't mean for it to end in a question to add questions.

Brandon nodded.

"I'll see you soon."

"I hope I do." Her mom waved.

Missy stayed quiet until they were a block down the street. "That was close. I've felt like my parents have been micro scoping me for weeks. Say I'm not looking healthy and pale."

"You've been looking pale."

"I know. I can't sleep." *I took two sleeping pills but I don't want Brandon to think his future girlfriend is on drugs. Well, I hope I'm his future girlfriend.*

"Why?"

"Can't explain."

"I might understand."

Missy exhaled, "I've been having nightmares almost every night. I got a prescription for a sleeping pill to help me sleep. Problem is, I still dream and can't wake up to stop the dreams. I'm scared to go to sleep."

"Has this whole backhoe and the driver the cause of it?" He put his hands in his back pockets.

"Funny, I heard my mom tell my dad I'm going through depression and don't know why. But since you moved here, it got worse."

"Why is that funny?" He kept his vision straight ahead, not looking at Missy.

"My mom called around and knows you're not a bad boy on drugs and use people."

"Nice to know."

"Seriously, don't worry. But it is funny right when you moved in, the backhoe went to work more than usual."

"I wonder if this is what my dad is working on." In silence, they walked down Ginger Lane and out of view from the front windows of Missy's house. "We'll go the back way to the shack so we aren't seen from the main road." Brandon reached for Missy's hand. She let him take it.

"We can get in serious trouble. What if someone is there?"

"First, we'll see if his car is around." Brandon pointed across the field. "And we'll only take a couple minutes to see what's down there. It has to be important for Jim or whoever to come back and take serious time to look for it."

"True. What if there's a trap and we're stuck or the cave collapses?"

Brandon tightened his grip on her hand. "No what ifs. We go, look, and scram."

They reached the end of Ginger Lane as the road curved to the right to the end of the field. A dirt road paralleled the houses' back yards. Missy was glad there were a few trees along the path to help block their presence.

"I can't believe we are doing this. If your dad finds out, we'll be in jail for life."

"I doubt the 'in jail for life', but he will be upset."

"Then why are we doing this?"

"I don't have to answer that. You know as much as I do, and we want to see what maybe my dad and the officers can't see."

The end of the trail was near, and the carport was empty except for the backhoe. "No car, no trouble," Brandon winked and headed to the shack. He reached the door, turned the knob and opened it. "All clear."

Jim had left the hole leading to the tunnel uncovered. Brandon turned on his cell phone flashlight and looked into the hole. Slowly, he backed down the wooden ladder.

"I'm not sure about this." Missy felt like miniature dogs were nipping in her stomach.

"The ladder's safe."

"Okay, I'm coming, I'm coming." Missy took her turn on the ladder. Brandon supported her back for the last few steps.

"See? You made it safe." They stood inches from each other, face to face. Dim daylight glowed on the floor from the shack above, lighting a four-foot view of the tunnel.

Missy rubbed her belly in a circular motion.

Brandon tilted his head. "Knots in your belly?"

"A little tight, yeah."

"Will this help?" Brandon drew her closer and gave her a soft kiss.

"Somewhat." Missy smiled at him. "Do you have any idea what's in here?"

"No, but we'll soon find out." He flashed his cell light around. "There are three tunnels, but it looks like they use the one on the left. I see a shovel leaning by the opening."

They were a few feet from the ladder when they heard a door creak open.

255

"What?" Missy whispered.

"Shhhhh."

They heard footsteps move to the hole in the floor. Brandon and Missy backed up to the tunnel wall.

Bang. The lid dropped and the tunnel went dark.

"Someone's up there. Maybe it's Jim. What if he comes down?" Missy whispered.

"We'll wait till he leaves, and then leave."

They stood for another ten minutes but knew Jim or someone else was still in the shack because of the sounds above. After a few minutes, it went quiet.

"I think we're safe. I'll go first," Brandon said. He stepped up the ladder and stopped when they heard another set of footsteps. Someone was talking.

***

"Hey, Jim, pal. Give me a hand with this," said a husky male voice.

"Hold your boxers, Dwight; I got to take care of something first."

The trapdoor lid rose and a flashlight beamed down into the hole. A set of feet came into view.

***

Brandon and Missy crept into the last tunnel and stopped. Neither knew where the tunnel ended or which way to go.

"I can't see. Get a brighter beam on your cell." Missy's voice was a ragged whisper.

"Not yet. They'll know someone's here. Move slow and quiet." Brandon found her hand. He touched the dirt wall to guide them deeper into the tunnel.

"How many tunnels are in here, Jim?" Dwight asked in a raised voice.

"Three I saw, but only one is open. I'm not going to break open walls unless needed to. Maybe there are more hidden treasures behind them, but it can wait for a later time."

"I'm not fond of being underground."

"It's worth it, my friend, it's worth it."

Missy yanked Brandon's sleeve. "They're coming this way. How are we going to hide?"

"We keep moving."

Footsteps followed quickly behind them. Brandon brightened his cell light and speed-walked until they reached a large open space. There were two openings like miniature caves inside the tunnel.

Brandon stopped. He turned a circle looking at the area. They couldn't see much. He took a step towards the cave, slipped on a small rock and caught himself.

***

"Did you hear something?" Dwight asked.

"Hear what?" On edge and having a bad day, Jim had developed a growing annoyance with Dwight's questions.

"I don't know, just a noise." Dwight looked around, nervous.

Jim shrugged. "A loose rock."

"I doubt it."

"What do you mean?"

"Ghosts."

"You got to be kidding me." Jim had about all he could take.

"No. There are rumors."

Jim stopped walking and turned to look at Dwight. "Go ahead," he said, sounding irritated by the whole thing. "Fill me in on those ghost rumors." *I know people believe in ghosts, but it's hard to believe one looks too human.*

Dwight shrugged. "People died building Nampa. They must like the place because they don't want to leave."

"Fine. I'll keep an eye out for a boogeyman. Now stop ghost yapping. Let's get the stuff and get out of here."

But Dwight kept talking. He got more animated as he went, gesturing with his hands in the beam of the flashlight he held which made shadows dance across the walls. "In the early morning, there's mist on the field, but it's not a mist. It's the spirits of the dead. Yes, indeed it is."

"Calm down, there's no such thing as ghosts." We have work to do, misty fields or not. Jim gestured to Dwight to zip it and follow him.

***

Missy listened to the two men talking. Jim and someone named Dwight. She whispered in Brandon's ear. "They're right behind us."

"Go in the side tunnel. I'm right behind you," Brandon whispered.

"But aren't they going to look in there?"

"No time. Go." He turned and pushed her into the side tunnel. They wedged themselves behind a casket and a stack of boxes.

***

"All right, Jim. Where are they?"

"See those shoulder-high caves? In there, those caskets should be full of Twist and everything else we need. Maybe some counterfeit money, too."

"We're taking it all?"

"We can't carry it all. We'll fill the duffle bags for now and come back in a couple of days."

Jim's light filled the opening where Melissa and Brandon were hiding.

"Sounds good to me," Dwight said with excitement. "Hope no ghosts will come after us."

"Stop it. Time to get serious. Hand me the crowbar."

"I thought you, had it?"

Jim lifted his hands, growing angry. "Do you see me holding it?" He turned back towards the entrance.

"Wait. Don't leave me."

"Scared a ghost is going come and get ya?"

Dwight wiped the sweat off his forehead. "You need help finding it."

"Hurry up," Jim murmured "You're a pain in the butt." The cave was dark and silent.

***

"They left for a minute. I need to see if there is another way out," Brandon said. "Fast."

They stood behind the casket, ducked under the wall, and tried to quick-walk without making noise. They didn't get much further when the two men were heard again.

Brandon guided Missy the opposite way. "Look, there's a different opening at the other end of this tunnel."

Missy hoped it wasn't a dead end. She'd had enough of hiding from trouble.

Dwight and Jim entered the open space by the cave as the teens reached the exit on the other side. It wasn't blocked. They went down a few feet and stopped. They could hear the faint talking again.

***

"You ever get the feeling of being watched?" Dwight asked.

"I'm going put you in the coffin and lock it if you don't stop talking about ghosts." Jim led Dwight into the smaller cave Brandon and Missy had just left.

"Whatever," Dwight griped. He took a crowbar and pried open the coffin lid. "Oh, yes. The mother lode. Your grandparents must have worked overtime." He chuckled. "I am going to enjoy myself. Yessirree. Old Dwight's heading for a few fun nights on the town."

"Don't let it be too many. People will notice a new Dwight and get suspicious. We don't want to attract any attention. Lay low. You hear me?"

Dwight nodded, but his mind was elsewhere. "I hear you."

"I hope you don't talk in your sleep."

"Nope. I sleep like a baby. I sleep like the dead." Dwight laughed at his joke.

"Fine. As long as you keep your yap shut."

"Jim, you got nothing to worry about. I'm not going to spill the beans. I'm tired of being broke, and if it means staying off the grid, I can do it."

"Good. Fill up the duffle and I'll do this one."

Jim opened his bag and stacked packages of twist in as tight as he could. He thought of giving his Arizona and Mexican people fifty percent of their money on this round. He would give them the rest after he made another trip back soon.

***

Missy could hear the men talking, but couldn't make out whole words. Something got in her nose and she twitched. It felt like a flea had flown into her sinuses, and she knew a sneeze was coming. She pinched her nostrils.

"Stop moving around," Brandon whispered and took a step further down the tunnel.

The pressure in her nose was building like a jet getting ready for take-off. Missy never held in a sneeze and they were loud. She inhaled deep breaths. It wasn't helping. This thing was ready to let loose.

"Huh, huh," She squeezed her nose tighter. "Ch-kish!"; A squeak escaped between her lips.

Brandon stopped, turned, and looked at her.

"Sorry."

***

"Noise again," Dwight said.

"Maybe you're right about ghosts." Jim took a step closer to the branching entrance. "Sounded like a sneeze."

"Ghosts can sneeze," Dwight said.

Jim gave a dry chuckle. "I'll look and see. You stay here and keep bagging up the goodies." *Was it Carlos? Did he find another entrance and was tracking me down? I wouldn't be surprised if he did.*

"Got it."

Jim stepped into the branch entrance. "Hello? Carlos? Anyone in here?" He waited and listened. "I hear something moving," he told Dwight.

***

"Keep going," Brandon said, and he tugged Missy's hand hard. She looked over her shoulder to see if there was any light following them.

"Come on." Brandon took a big step and Missy lost his hand.

She turned back again to look, too fast, and ran into the wall. She bounced away, hitting the ground and landing on her side.

Missy managed to sit up and looked around. "Brandon," she whispered aloud. It was pitch dark except for the small light she saw on Brandon's cell a few feet away. She rested her head on her knees.

"Where are you?" Brandon said in a soft voice.

"I'm sitting on the floor where you left me. Hurry." She saw a bright light coming down the tunnel. A hand rested on her arm. She jerked up in a sitting position.

"Sorry." Brandon helped Missy up. The light was getting closer.

"I thought it was you and found a better app for your cell."

"It's not me and we don't have time to run."

The bright light lit the teens and Missy flung herself on Brandon.

"Is that you, Carlos, with a friend?" the voice asked. He adjusted the light on his hardhat to shine down lower. He took a few more steps to get a closer look. Brandon wrapped his arms around Missy. She saw the man's face and knew it was Jim.

"Don't scream, I'm not going to hurt you." Jim kept his gaze on Missy and did not notice Brandon. "Not a safe place to be, you know." He ran his hand through her hair once. Missy winced. Brandon tightened his grip and drew her back a step.

"Either I'm having déjà vu or you're Violet's daughter." He took a small bag out of his pocket and sniffed. "Want some Twist? It's good stuff and gives you all the energy you need."

Missy squeaked as Brandon pulled her to his side further down the tunnel.

"Trying to escape? People get lost in these tunnels." Jim sniffed some more and turned around.

"You know where your mom put my ring. Did she name you Violet after her?"

"I'm Missy. Melissa."

Brandon took another step with her, out of Jim's reach.

"I don't know about a ring." *I'm not sure if Brandon is thinking to take a run for it or stay. This guy is freaking me out but I feel a connection. Why?*

"Yes, you do. Where is it? It's the promise ring I gave you, for us. We were to be together, Vee."

"I'm not Violet."

"Stop messing with me. We were the best perfect couple ever, especially with my ring on your finger." Jim ran his hand down the side of Missy's head again. She shivered.

"I wouldn't move. My big boss could be down here too. He's the one with the gun." He got closer. "Why did you drop me for Ray, VeVe? Remember me calling you 'VeVe'? It was your name I gave you." His hand moved down her arm and closed around it.

Missy was scared and speechless. She held onto Brandon with a death grip.

"Come on, VeVe. You know what I'm talking about." His eyes seemed to drain the energy out of her.

"I … I don't have it."

"What do you mean? I'm sure you pretended to throw it. I bet it's in a special place. It's the ring I gave to you. For us." He got closer to Missy as Brandon didn't know if to pull her back.

A mist rose behind Jim. Missy pointed with her free hand. Jim looked puzzled. He turned; his expression changed when he saw the haze drifting towards them. He still held her arm.

Missy saw a figure come out of the mist. It was a Native American. It looked like the picture of the warrior she had seen at the library. The look on his face was not friendly.

Jim acted like he had forgotten Missy and Brandon were there. He let go of her arm, turned around and went back down the tunnel, the same way he came.

The mist faded and was gone.

Missy felt like she was in a cold storage meat locker. She shivered. *He had called me 'Violet'. Proof, Jim Forst is alive.*

Brandon held her tighter. "What in the hell was that?" Missy turned, buried her head against his chest and cried

***

"See anything?" Dwight asked. He had finished stuffing the duffels when Jim returned.

"I think I've sniffed a little too much Twist. I'm on the edge and now, seeing the ghosts you believe exists. I'm starting to get claustrophobic." He looked around, taking in his surroundings, and felt a bit better.

"Ghosts? You saw ghosts?"

"Whatever it was, it's gone now. Let's move it." Jim questioned what he had seen, but didn't want to ponder. First important thing was to get out of this place on the road to Arizona. They would eat and sleep on beds with decent padding. He and Dwight would be traveling with three duffle bags full of Twist.

"Here's the first bag." Dwight tossed it to Jim.

Jim's anxiousness was quieting. The image of the girl had faded. The mist dissipated. Not enough oxygen, he guessed, or maybe just breathing old air.

Dirt drizzled on top of them. Dwight looked up. "Either an earthquake is coming or more ghosts are coming." He sounded dazed.

"Time for us to go." Jim hurried with the other bags.

"Right. Time to go," Dwight repeated, as he swept his flashlight around for one last look. "Let's hurry up."

Jim took a couple of steps towards the entrance of the cave. He was done with these tunnels, these bones, stories of ghosts, mists, and even Violet. He smiled as he hefted the duffle over his shoulder. A new way of life was in his hands.

Chapter 38

"We've got to get out of here. There should be an exit around here somewhere," Brandon said as he kept one arm around Missy and used the other to guide them with his cell phone. "My battery is running out."

Missy felt a little woozy from clocking herself into the wall, but she walked along with Brandon. The tunnel had a couple of blind turns, but Missy stayed on her feet. Finally, after the last turn, Missy beckoned, "Stop. Please stop." She bent over to catch her breath.

"Sorry, Missy. I know your hurting, but we got to get out of here. What if Jim and his friend come back to get us?"

"I want to go home." She stood up and they continued walking. He gave her a quick squeeze and Missy knew they both hoped to find an exit soon. Another ten minutes of silent walking went by until they came to a T in the tunnel.

"Which way?" Missy panicked as she looked to the right and left.

"I don't know. This is frustrating." He walked in the path on the right for a few steps and the tunnel ended. "Nothing here."

"Go left and we'll try it."

After a short walk, they saw a dim light. A door. The wood wasn't fitted well and light came through the cracks. They reached the door and Missy tried the handle. "It's unlocked but something is blocking it. Now what?"

"Let me try." Brandon took the handle and pushed on the door. Nothing. It wouldn't budge.

Missy turned around and banged on the door with her fists. "I'm tired of this. Help!" She kept hammering on the wood. "Get us out!"

"Calm down."

"What do you mean calm down. I was handled by a crook, ran into a wall, and now locked in a tunnel." She screamed and bashed the door again. She stiffened. He tried to move her out of the way but she didn't budge.

"Let us out! Help! Please help! Let us out!" Missy switched to her feet and kicked.

They heard a female voice call back. "Hello? Who's there?"

"Please, we're trapped and someone's after us!" Missy cried.

"Hold on a minute," the voice called.

"I'm scared," Missy said.

Brandon rested his head on hers. "I think this haunted maze is over."

The voice called out again. "You there?"

"Yes, get us out," Brandon called.

"I'm working on it. Lots of boxes blocking the door. I have to move them." Sounds of clunks and banging carried on for what seemed hours, the door opened a few inches. "There's enough room for you to squeeze in. There are boxes behind the door."

It was easy for Missy to squeeze through the gap, but Brandon had to push the weight of the packed boxes on the door an inch to make it through.

"Thank you," Missy stood there and cried like a baby. Brandon hugged her again as she shook.

"I'm Ruth. How did you get in the tunnel under my store? Never mind. Follow me up the stairs to break room." She led them to the back of her store. Brandon and Missy sat on a love seat and the Ruth brought her tissues. "There you go." She sat at a nearby chair. "What were you doing?"

Sirens blasted down the street. Missy looked at Brandon and wondered if they had just caught Jim and Dwight.

Ruth looked towards the front of her shop and back at the kids. She raised an eyebrow as if wondering if the sirens were the reason, they were hiding or running away. "Are you in trouble? Are you hiding?"

"Hard to explain," Brandon replied. He took his cell phone out of his pocket and saw the battery had died. He put it back.

"Did you say someone was after you? Do we need to call the police? Tell them you're here and safe?"

Ruth looked Missy over. "Is she injured?" She looked at Brandon. "Scratches on her forehead and blood on her

269

hands. Do I need to call the ambulance? What happened down there? How did you get there? Where have you been?"

Brandon shook his head. "She'll be fine. We're in enough trouble as it is. Could you take us home?"

Missy's eyes were dilated and she felt dizzy. She guessed she had hit the wall harder than she realized.

Ruth eyed them both. Missy wondered if she felt they were the cause of danger. They were running for safety. Somehow, they had to make her understand that.

Ruth looked at her watch. "I'll close shop and take you home." She looked at Missy. "The bathroom is around the corner. There's a washcloth you can use to clean yourself up. You might have a splinter or two in your hands."

Missy got up on rubbery legs. Too rubbery. She lost her balance and fell, close to hitting her head on the corner of the coffee table.

"Missy!" Brandon yelped and caught her before she hit the floor.

Ruth knelt beside her. "Can you sit?" She placed her hand behind Missy's back and helped her up to the couch again. "Do I need to call 911?" She reached for the phone.

"Don't call, please." Missy was worried and hurting, but she was more embarrassed.

"Need help?" Brandon scooted to the edge of the couch.

"No, no. I can make it." Missy constrained herself up and wove her way to the bathroom.

Missy closed the door as she heard Ruth pick up the phone and dial. "Winnie, this is Ruth. I'm closing shop an hour early. I'll tell you about it later. My dad? I have no idea where he went. I've got to go. I'll see you tomorrow." Ruth hung up the phone. "Fixed. Let's go."

Brandon told Ruth where he lived and she drove them to his house. Neither he nor Missy said a single word the whole way. But, when they got out, she followed suit.

"I'm not dropping you off without knowing what you're up to. I smell trouble and sense you two are not the cause," Ruth said. Missy looked at Brandon; they were in no position to argue.

"Mom?" Brandon called when they entered the house.

"Coming," Mrs. Miller rounded the corner into the vestibule; her eyes widened when she saw Ruth standing behind the kids.

"What's going on? Where were you?" She glanced over at Missy and Brandon. Missy was pale and dirty from taking the spill inside the tunnel. Brandon looked dusty himself. "Brandon?"

Brandon didn't answer.

"We've called your cell numerous times and you didn't answer. Not good. Again, what's going on?" Brandon's mom at first focused on the kids, and then looked to Ruth behind them. "Oh, I'm sorry. Have these teens caused you trouble?"

"I'm Ruth. I run the antique store downtown. I don't think they've done anything wrong except being where they shouldn't." She nodded to them. "They said someone chased them, but from where, I don't know."

"Being chased?" Brandon's mom repeated. Missy watched her look at their dirty clothes and add two and two together. "Your mother has called several times looking for you."

"Please call and say Missy's here," Brandon said. "Ask them to come over. Is Dad here?"

"I'll call Melissa's mother and yes, your dad is here, and he's not happy." Mrs. Miller walked to the staircase and called down the stairs. "Dean, the kids are back."

"On my way." They heard his shoes hit the stairs harder than normal on his way up. He stood by his wife and looked Brandon over carefully. "You were given permission to be gone an hour and you've been gone half the day."

Brandon raised his hand for pause. "Not now, Dad, please. Wait for Missy's parents to get here."

Missy watched Brandon and his father exchange looks. It appeared, despite his anger, he was going to wait. Mrs. Miller got a pitcher of water and a stack of glasses. She set them on the table. "Take a seat," She gestured to the table, went back into the kitchen, and came out with a jar of cookies. They gathered around the table and sat. Brandon scooted his chair close to Missy and held her hand.

Mr. Miller nodded to the jar. "Go on. You two must be hungry."

Mrs. Miller saw the Mack's walking up the driveway. "Looks like your parents are here, Missy."

Brandon and Missy nibbled on cookies when Mrs. Miller opened the door. Mrs. Mack ran over to Missy and Mr. Mack followed.

"Melissa, you're hurt."

"I'm fine. I sort of ran into a wall and knocked myself on the head."

Missy's mom noticed her daughter was holding Brandon's hand. She looked at Ruth. "Did they break something in your store?"

"Oh, no. I let them in my store from the basement," Ruth explained.

"The tunnel?" Brandon's dad asked.

Brandon and Missy nodded.

"How did you get in there?" *If looks could kill.* He glared hard at them; Missy thought his eyes would burn right through Brandon.

"Dad, let me explain. Missy's been having bad nightmares." Missy nodded in agreement. "I know you told us not to go to the shack, but we did. We found an opening in the floor and it led down into the tunnel." Brandon was having a hard time keeping eye contact with his dad. He let go of Missy's hand and folded his arms. "Jim Forst is alive. I mean, someone named Dwight called him Jim. It's got to be the same guy. They kept drugs and bogus money inside the coffins buried in the tunnels."

"How do you know about Jim? He's dead." Mrs. Mack's voice quivered, as if not wanting her first love still alive. Mr. Mack rubbed her back to calm her down. "I've got to sit," she took the seat across from Missy.

273

Brandon took a drink of water, got a cookie and put it back down. "Missy and I knew there was something fishy going on. We didn't know if it had anything to do with Jim. We were in the old shack and found an old newspaper on the wall and an old picture of Mrs. Mack stuck in the corner."

Mr. Miller stared hard at both of them. Missy thought the floor would open beneath her.

"Dad. I'm telling you what we found. We didn't know anything. I wanted to show Missy it was real people messing around, not a so-called ghost. Going for joyrides at night on a backhoe, stupid stuff, and it didn't have to be anything bad. I wanted to help her so she could stop having nightmares about it."

"You told Brandon about your nightmares and not me? I'm the one who hears you tossing and turning at night. It's me who comes in and hugs you. I'm the one that rushed you to ER thinking you had a seizure. So why didn't you tell me?" Mrs. Mack sounded hurt.

Missy lowered her head. "I didn't think you'd understand."

She took a deep breath. "I don't know what to say."

Mr. Miller continued on as if there was no interruption, "You found out, Brandon? You found the link to Twist?"

Brandon hung his head for a minute. "Yes, sir." He looked up. "I wanted to show Missy not to be afraid."

Missy's mom's voice mixed with anger and worry. "While you were in the tunnel it could've collapsed on the two of you."

Brandon opened his mouth, but no words came out.

"Why did you go down there?" Mr. Miller asked.

Missy answered for Brandon. "We went for a peek. I mean, it was kind of cool. We know there are tunnels underneath Nampa, but I've never been in one."

Brandon looked at Missy and back at his dad. "After we found the hole, we snooped around. Yes, we were snooping."

"You disobeyed my direct order not to go there."

Brandon nodded. "Yes Dad."

He blew out a deep breath. "Go on."

"There are three tunnels. Two only went in a few feet before it ended. The third, the one in the middle, is where we were going along when we heard the trap door shut at the top of the ladder. After that, we knew we had to keep going."

Missy couldn't let him take the blame. "I wanted to see, too. We kept going but we heard people behind us. They said 'Twist is in the coffins.'"

Brandon nodded. "It is."

"Did you see it?" Mr. Miller asked.

Brandon shook his head. "But we heard a little before we got too far away."

"This gets worse and worse," Mr. Miller said to Mrs. Miller.

She nodded. "You realize you put Missy in danger, Brandon. Those men are criminals. Criminals do not care who they hurt. Do you understand?"

"I do now."

Mrs. Mack folded her hands.

Brandon continued the story. "The guys came down the ladder. We had to get away, so Missy and I went further into the main tunnel. I think this Jim guy knew we were there, or thought it was a person named Carlos. He followed us for a couple of minutes. We got away. We found a door and Ruth let us in."

Mr. Miller gave a grateful nod to Ruth. "Did you get the name of the other man?"

"Dwight?" Brandon looked at Missy.

"Yes."

"Are you positive the other man's name was Dwight?" Ruth waited for the worse.

They both nodded.

Ruth's face went pale. "You're talking about my dad."

"Stay here. I've got to make a few calls," Mr. Miller went back to his office.

Missy's dad, who had been silent the whole time, spoke up. "You know better." He looked at his daughter's messy hair and scratches on her forehead and body. "Who knows what could've happened." Missy could tell he held back a yell.

"Or killed," her mom said.

Mrs. Miller raised her shoulders and hands in dismay. "You were foolish, the two of you. You don't know how much danger you were in."

"But Jim didn't hurt me," Missy said in her defense and folded her arms.

Her mom's eyes narrowed, "What do you mean Jim didn't hurt you?"

Crap, I let the cat out of the bag and now I need to come up with something.

"It was when I hit my head on the wall. My head hurts bad. Brandon helped me up as there was a light getting brighter in the tunnel. It was him. Jim. He's alive, Mom. But he didn't do anything. He, he was nice."

"And?" Brandon's dad entered the room again.

"He kept sniffing powder and saying I looked like mom. Then he started calling me Vivi or something like that." Missy reached for her glass of water and took her time drinking with small sips.

"And?" He asked with more firmness.

"Dwight called to him and he left."

"He left?"

Missy nodded. *They'd think I was crazy for telling them about the Native American ghost I saw.*

"It was like he forgot I was there. He walked away and I got the heck out of there with Brandon."

"We found the end of the tunnel. The basement door to Ruth's place." Brandon looked at her.

"Right. It's an old door. I had boxes stacked in front to block it. I've checked out the tunnel from my door before and didn't want to be reminded of it again. Creepy place."

Mr. Miller gave the kids a stern look. "Brandon, you and I are going to have a serious talk. But, Melissa, I think your parents will have a few choice words for you, too."

Missy's parents agreed.

He turned to Ruth. "Your dad owns a used car lot?"

"Yes."

"What's the name of the place?"

"Hartley's Auto."

"Police got a call for a break-in and robbery. The lobby/office was ransacked; money and usable license plates were taken."

"Did they find the robbers? Is my dad okay?" Ruth asked.

"Nobody was there. You can't go there now while it's under investigation."

Mrs. Miller rested her hand on Ruth's back as if she didn't know what else to do.

Missy sighed.

Chapter 39

Mr. Miller texted a few messages and looked at Ruth. "What other business has your dad been in?"

"None. He sells cars. But he's never done anything wrong."

"Do you live with your parents?" He was writing notes in his small notebook.

"Heck no. My mom passed away years ago and I don't see my dad much." Ruth raised her eyebrows.

"Does Dwight have any gambling problems you know of?"

"Plays cards with his buddies. Penny ante stuff. I never noticed anything."

Mr. Miller kept writing. "I know this is hard. We'll talk with you soon."

Ruth nodded, looking worried. "In the meantime, I'll call a few places. Someone might have seen him."

"Let me know."

Ruth nodded again and took another drink.

"I need to make more phone calls and have to go to the police station when we're done." Mr. Miller headed back to his office again.

Brandon and Missy knew they were in major hot water. But they weren't going anywhere. Missy's dad went to pick up Tommy at their neighbor's; it looked like they would stay longer at the Miller's house. Tommy was excited when they got back to the Miller's. He didn't mind having a room to himself playing games and watching movies.

Mrs. Miller got him set up with a bowl of popcorn and a small plate of cookies. "Come see me if you want anything." Tommy smiled and nodded.

They sat in the living room waiting for Mr. Miller to return. Brandon sat by Missy on the couch and her parents on the other side. Mrs. Miller sat in a chair, watching Brandon and Missy. She managed to keep a conversation going about school and what classes they liked.

Mr. Miller came back again with a beeper on his hip, took a seat and looked at Missy's parents. "Can you tell me full details of what happened fifteen years ago with Jim's accident?"

Mrs. Mack agreed. "Back when we were in high school, besides the Parade of America and the Snake River Stampede, we had a yearly Potato Celebration." Missy's dad situated himself in the chair.

"In the field by the dirt pit was where it was held. Dances, country music, all sorts of celebration activities." He took a sip of his water. "The tractor race was like a

280

relay race of some sort. We would drive the tractors to a pile of dirt, lift a scoopful with the front bucket, and race to the pit to dump it. A rope ran across the field by the pit, so we knew when to stop and dump the dirt with no harm.

Mr. Miller leaned forward in his chair. "Tractor races?"

"Yes, for countless years. Nobody got hurt."

"What type of tractors?" Mrs. Miller asked.

Mr. Mack paused for a second, then to the wall. "David Brown brand. First year in 1989. There used to be John Deere, but they decided to use a different brand. I couldn't see too much of a difference."

Brandon's dad opened his notebook again and quickly had a pen in hand. "Can you tell me all you remember?"

Missy's parents looked at each other with remorseful feelings.

"The last race we ran went bad," Mr. Mack said. "Jim was behind me when I was on the way to dump the dirt. I backed up and Jim bumped into me. His front loader was full of dirt, but not lifted. It was tilted and the dirt fell out. I tried to move forward a bit, but couldn't. I was over the warning rope. Any further I would have fallen into the pit."

"You think Jim bumped into you on purpose?"

Missy's parents looked at Mrs. Miller again and sighed. "Yes."

"What happened next?"

"I'll never forget it. Jim throttled his tractor full force, with the lift facing me. It looked like teeth getting ready to bite me." Mr. Mack rubbed his forehead. "He must have been focused on me. He didn't watch where he was going. Next thing, he was falling into the pit."

"Any reason why Jim would want to hurt you?"

"Personal stuff." Mrs. Mack's voice softened. Missy saw the color had drained out of her face.

Mrs. Miller showed concern. "Let me get you a glass of cold water." She hurried into the kitchen and came back with a full glass with ice added. "Here."

"Thank you." Mrs. Mack held the glass but didn't drink it. "Jim and I, we liked each other. We dated for a while. I broke up with him right before the last race." She put the glass on the coffee table and rubbed her hands together. "I met Ray and was going to give Jim back his ring. But we fought and I pretended to throw it in the pit instead. It was a mean thing to do. It was a friendship ring." She wasn't looking at anything while she explained. Lifting the glass, she took a big swallow. "The breakup made him angry. I picked a bad time to tell him, but I didn't want to see him anymore. After the race would have been better."

Missy could feel the pain in her mother's voice.

"And you attended the funeral?" Mr. Miller asked.

"I didn't," Mr. Mack said, "but Violet went. He wasn't buried in Nampa. They have family in Arizona and his body was shipped there. The family plot, I think."

Mr. Miller scribbled on his notebook.

Mrs. Mack, who still stared at the wall, had a little color back on her face.

Mr. Mack continued. "He was trying to push me. I didn't know the tractor could flip."

Tears ran down Mrs. Mack's face. "It wasn't a race anymore. He tried to kill Ray."

Missy was biting her lower lip and fighting off her tears of mixed feelings. "Mom, how many of the people in your 4H group had the same jacket design?"

"Four." She hiccupped with a cry.

"I saw a guy wearing a jacket like yours at the parade."

"Maybe he got it at a yard sale or a thrift store?" Brandon's mom asked.

Mrs. Mack shrugged. "Anything's possible."

"In any case, Jim is dead." Missy's dad said.

"We believe he isn't." The way Mr. Miller said 'we' made them look at him. Missy's eyes opened wider in shock. Brandon kept the same plain face with no emotion.

Missy's mom buried her face in her hands.

The center of attention, Mr. Miller took a long, deep breath, as if deciding how much more he should reveal. "We have reason to believe Jim is alive, and his family's drugs and bogus money racket is still operating. I can't go into the details even though you know most of it." He looked at each of them and pointed towards the room Tommy was in as he spoke their names, "You set foot again at the shack or pit, I'll put both of you in a safe house far, far away. The whole area is now off-limits," Mr. Miller said. "Understand?" Brandon sat still. Missy nodded.

Tommy came back to the table asking for another cookie. "I like your cookies," he rubbed his stomach at Mrs. Miller.

"Thank you."

Tommy looked up at Mr. Miller. "Do you think the Native Chief knows the bad man?" he asked.

Brandon's dad looked carefully at the faces in the room. "I don't know what the Native Chief knows. But now is not a good time to ask him."

Tommy nodded.

Mr. Miller's pager beeped and he excused himself. He came back up with the news. "There is a police warrant to search Dwight's house and his business."

Ruth didn't say anything. Missy felt bad for her.

"We're also going to search the Forst Funeral Home, the shack, and the tunnels." Mr. Miller slipped on his jacket. "I need to leave for work." He kissed Mrs. Miller. She watched him leave.

"We need to leave, too," said Mr. Mack, standing. "Rita, thank you. Ruth…" His voice trailed. Ruth nodded and left, holding back tears of her own.

Brandon was Missy's shadow out to the car. Tommy was sound asleep. His dad carried him out and laid him in the back seat. Tommy had watched movies and left no traces of popcorn or cookies in the bowls. They drove home in silence. All Missy could think of was the ghost… and Jim Forst's sea blue eyes.

***

Tired, Mrs. Mack put Tommy to bed and called Missy into her room.

"Where's Dad?"

She motioned for Missy to close the door. "In his office."

Missy only nodded and said nothing.

"I want to talk to you about what happened today, but I'm too numb at the moment. However, I do want to show you something." Missy's mom went into her walk-in closet. Missy sat on the bed and heard a drawer open and shut. She came back out holding a small box in her hands.

"What's in there?"

Mrs. Mack sat beside her. "The ring Jim gave me when we were dating in high school." She held the box like it was fragile. "I haven't looked at it for years." She lowered the box to her lap and opened the lid with ease. A blue gem ring sparkled.

"It's like there's a tiny light bulb in it," Missy said.

"It's called a star sapphire. The light is what makes the stone special. This is a small one. Jim gave it to me. He said it's the color of his eyes."

They look like my eyes, too. Missy thought. Her mom took it out and placed it on the ring finger of her right hand. "This hand is for friendship," she said. "The left is for, you know. It still fits. I know he wanted it to be for my left hand, but..." She sighed and turned the ring in circles on her finger. "I liked Jim a lot but he was a troubled boy. For a while, I thought, since we liked each other, the trouble would go away." She looked away. "Trouble followed... still follows Jim." She shook her head. Looking at Missy, she asked, "Want to try it on?"

"No way."

She nodded with a small smile. "Good girl."

"What are you going to do with it?"

Mrs. Mack pulled the ring off and placed it back in the box. "Give it back. I want Jim Forst out of our family's life for good. I was spiteful. I'm not proud of what I did. I should have waited." She sighed. "I should have waited."

"But Jim's alive, Mom."

"Yes, he is. Not easy news."

"How are you going to give it back?" Missy watched her mom rub the box. "Dad doesn't want any of us to go anywhere near the shack. And besides, he's gone. They said they were leaving."

"You heard a lot, little lady, for someone who didn't hear what Dwight and Jim were planning."

Missy shrugged. "I heard a little. You can't hear too well in those tunnels."

"I see." Mrs. Mack gave her another smile. "I'm going to go somewhere I shouldn't and put it back in the last place I saw him, the tractor. Our little secret?" Mom raised her eyebrows. "He'll either find it or he won't. But if he does go looking, he'll know." Missy's mom stood and held out her hand to Missy. She took the offer and gave her a tight hug. "I need to say my last goodbye to Jim." She left Missy standing in her room as she walked through the house and closed the front door behind her.

Chapter 40

Two days after the scare in the tunnel, Brandon visited Missy often. She thought his dad might forbid it, or her mom would, but could see Brandon was a good kid.

The stress at the Miller's was building up; Brandon's dad was busy nonstop. Meetings were held in his office with the Special Agents looking for Jim and Dwight. Brandon said they had all kinds of maps up. Said it looked like a detective's office from a T.V. show.

Missy had often assumed it was for show. *Guess not.*

When it came to punishment for disobeying, their parents said Brandon's and Melissa's trouble and fright were enough. The kids had helped find clues the authorities weren't sure of. So, in some way, they sped up the search.

In the middle of the week, Mr. Miller came over and told Missy's parents they got half a dozen coffins out of the tunnel. Then, with special metal detectors, the officers found the rest of the laundered money and Twist during another dig. It looked like a 'who can dig the biggest hole in the field' contest to Missy.

No one had seen Jim or Dwight, nor had the authorities found them. Jim's parents were tracked down in Arizona and insisted they knew nothing about Jim's whereabouts. They had gotten away. For now. Missy knew Ruth was sad. Dwight was her dad.

Missy and Julie talked on the phone and hung out more often, even when Brandon was over. Their news about being prohibited from going anywhere near the shack or the dirt pit was fine with her. Julie agreed. Planet Mars would be too close.

Julie wanted to drag Missy to town and get a Peanut Buster Parfait. Funny, though. Missy's mom drove them to the drive-in and had to pass the misty field. It gave Missy a major shiver. More to the fact was, the field lay across the street from her house, but she was happy the shack was on the other side of the field at a safe distance.

Maura and Ally came over once, which surprised Missy a bit. They wanted to see how she was doing. But the real reason was to tell her Maura's family was moving to Murphy, before school in the fall. They asked if Missy had any new bruises. She showed them her legs and arms, but nothing new since Missy hit her head in the tunnel. They didn't ask Missy how it happened, so she was sure they knew all the details. How? Missy decided she would never know.

With Maura gone, Missy wondered if Ally would want to hang out more and become closer friends. It wouldn't bother her a bit if Ally didn't. Missy had Julie and

Brandon. They treated her like an important person, not a ghost.

***

Floating in the air like a balloon, feeling the freedom of space, Missy drifted through thin sheets of clouds and glided with a group of seagulls. The birds must have heard a noise because they scattered and disappeared.

Missy felt pressure on her back. Her flying decreased in speed. Maybe if she flapped harder, she'd get the pressure off. The weight got heavier. She felt hot and lost altitude.

The wind rushed past Missy's face as she headed toward the ground. She knew a crash was coming fast.

"Melissa, wake up." Her mom rubbed her back. "You've been asleep for hours and missed dinner."

"You made me fall."

"You haven't fallen. You're fine besides missing dinner. Oh, Brandon is coming over."

"What?"

"Brandon stopped by while you were sleeping." Her mom said. "Fifteen minutes until he comes back."

"Ugh." Missy wanted to go back to dreamland. It had been a long time since she hadn't had a nightmare.

She got up, dressed, and gave herself a cursory look in the mirror. *Not bad for a near-sixteen-year-old.* The doorbell rang and she headed down the hall. Brandon waited in the entryway with Missy's mom.

"We won't be gone too long, Mrs. Mack. I promise, no wandering in tunnels or any other strange places."

Her reply was a cautionary look and a slight nod.

"We'll be fine, mom." They headed out the door. "Any particular place you want to go?" asked Missy. They were going in the pit's direction.

Brandon didn't answer. Instead, he kissed her.

"I guess you like me."

"In a scary way." He smiled.

"Hey." She slapped his arm.

"Ouch. That hurt!"

"It did not." Missy rested her face on his shoulder. He drew her closer as they reached the top of the pit and observed the tractor.

"Here we are," he said.

"Aren't we supposed to stay away?"

"It's been a couple of weeks and no sign of Jim or Dwight."

"Your father may kill you, but why are we here?"

"Curious. I want to see if your mom's ring is still in the tractor."

"I forgot. I've blocked out anything to do with Jim."

"Please?" Brandon held out his hand. "Won't take long."

Missy shrugged. "I guess."

Stepping through the rubbish, they made it down the hill. The tractor looked the same. "Did she tell you where she put it?"

"No. I'll look here; you go on the other side."

Missy heard Brandon crunch the trash on his way around. The tractor door groaned as he opened it.

"Got it."

"The ring is there?"

"No. It's your mom's jacket."

"Are you serious?"

"It looks like her jacket to me. Isn't this the one you left behind in the shack?"

She circled the tractor and took it out of his hand. "How the heck did it get here?"

"There's a note. Let's see." He opened a piece of paper.

"Read it." She hugged the jacket tight.

Brandon laughed.

"What's funny?"

"The note, it says: 'About time,' and signed 'J'." He handed it to her.

"Nothing else?"

It was from Jim. They both knew it.

"He came back and checked the tractor. How did he know my mom put the ring there?"

"Who knows? The point is he came, found it, and he left the jacket."

"Stress off my back." Missy put the jacket on and stuck Jim's note in the pocket. "Can we go now?" She took a few steps towards the path and turned to Brandon, who was behind her. Something caught her eye above the tractor. A kind of mist. It was floating.

"*We thank you*," a voice said.

"What did you say?" Missy turned to Brandon because she thought he had spoken. No, it couldn't be right.

"I didn't say anything." He looked over his shoulder where Missy was staring. The mist cleared away. She turned and found her way up to the hard pavement of the road.

When she looked back, the misty figure was still there, hovering over the tractor. Missy remembered the photograph in the book at the library. It was the same face.

The first time it happened was at night in the ditch. Next, in the tunnel. But this time, it was right in front of her. Misty, like a ghost. A real ghost.

"What did you hear?" Brandon asked.

"A ghost."

"Right," he replied.

"I mean it," she pointed. "He's there."

The warrior looked straight at Missy. She had the idea he was happy and listened:

"I am John Badger Tso'ape-ha. I am John Badger Ghost."

"He's a Native American warrior," said Missy.

On his head was a badger skull. It made him look fierce. *Nice hat*, she thought at him. He smiled back.

"Aishenda'qa." Thank you…they rest in peace.

Brandon hugged Missy.

They could still see Tso'ape-ha on top of the tractor as Brandon pulled Missy away from the edge of the pit. It was time to leave. Missy took one last look and saw the ghost still there, watching them.

"You saw him, too?"

Brandon paused like he didn't want to admit it. At last, he nodded. "I saw him."

"Good." She turned back to confirm her sight. He was there, standing tall and quiet, a shadow blending into the dark.

Missy Mack's Adventure series continues with book two, Buried Secrets. The release date is September 2024.

Missy moves in with her once BF Maura Derringer and her family to join the Owyhee County gymnastics team.

Not a good choice. Someone is warning her to go home. After hiking the beautiful area around the Snake River in Idaho, she comes across clues that lead her to suspect Jim, Missy's mom's boyfriend from high school, is back in town making drugs.

To top it off, her past nightmares are back in action, including Starr Wilkinson/Bigfoot, racing the train on his ghost horse. Is she going to be safe enough to compete in gymnastics? Or should she heed the warnings?

.

Enjoyed the book? Let others know! Share thoughts and leave a positive review, please. Thank you.

Amazon:
https://www.amazon.com/stores/author/B08NJ81CFM/

Facebook:
https://www.facebook.com/jsmithandersen/
https://www.facebook.com/melissamackadventure/
https://www.facebook.com/thedenimblues

Etsy:
https://www.etsy.com/shop/Denimbluesco

Blog:
http://jsmithandersen.allauthor.com/

Twitter:
https://twitter.com/snapgrowl

LinkedIn:
https://www.linkedin.com/in/jsmithandersen/

Skool:
https://www.skool.com/denim-blues-self-healing-3251